The Power To Make A Choice

T0319127

Sr. Elizabeth Ngozi Okpalaenwe

Langaa Research & Publishing CIG
Mankon, Bamenda

Publisher
Langaa RPCIG
Langaa Research & Publishing Common Initiative Group
P.O. Box 902 Mankon
Bamenda
North West Region
Cameroon
Langaagrp@gmail.com
www.langaa-rpcig.net

Distributed in and outside N. America by African Books Collective
orders@africanbookscollective.com
www.africanbookcollective.com

ISBN: 9956-726-30-3

DISCLAIMER
All views expressed in this publication are those of the author and do not necessarily reflect the views of Langaa RPCIG.

You, Not Others

Do you ever laugh at yourself and laugh with others?
 Look at your short comings and empathize with others?
 Acknowledge your limitations and commend others?
 You can only give what you have to others.

How often do you complement yourself and others?
Accept your mistakes, and excuse others?
Take responsibility for your actions and free others?
Every choice demands price from you and not others.

Your life leads you near or far from others,
Your choices can invite or scare others,
The rhyme of your music belongs to you and never to others,
The Power to make a choice belongs to you and not others.

Respect yourself and stand by others,
For unity stands while division scares others,
Often our story begins where it connects with others,
Your world begins when it creates room for others.

Selfishness erupts as you hide your gifts from others,
Look within and share your gifts with others,
You are your own happiness and cheering belongs to others,
The rule is Love to yourself and then others.

Acknowledgments

I am immensely grateful to God for His unwavering love and mercy that has always sustained me, especially throughout the period of my writing. I can never appreciate Him enough.

Next, I wish to express sincere gratitude to Mr Tangyie Peter Suh-Nfor and Dr John Niba Ndongmanji who appreciated and edited this work- for their time, ideas and useful advice.

I am highly indebted to Pauline Mason, for her invaluable assistance and care and to Ruth Roberts for proof reading it at the early stages of my writing. Both of them showed a rare promptness to participate and made useful corrections.

My profound gratitude equally goes to my lecturer, Mrs Sarah Bower, for her intuitive challenges, criticism, support that helped me while I was writing this novel throughout the period of my studies in Norwich.

To my colleagues of the University of East Anglia, Norwich, I offer profuse appreciation for their generous time they spent with me during lectures, helping with useful ideas and suggestions.

May God bless you all abundantly.

Foreword

The Power to Make a Choice, highlights the question of choice in human life in a very innovative manner. In the preface to his *Homage and Courtship*, Shadrach Ambanasom writes, "To prescribe only politics and proscribe any other subject matter would be to kill our creative spirit, to stultify our imaginative efforts and to truncate our Literature." Elizabeth Ngozi Okpalaenwe attempts an eclectic approach to the debate on subject matter in creative writing in her novel. Major concerns about Cameroon's political landscape which feature in the works of a number of preceding writers, are reiterated with a new voice. These include, brain drain, the antipathy between French speaking and English speaking Cameroonians, partisan politics, election squabbles, unemployment, the judiciary, the economy, the cancerous bribery and corruption and many more.

These issues are developed as the main story of Joe's family life unfolds. The kick-off conflict between Joe and his wife, Mary, over the education of their children sets in motion a series of squabbles, battles for survival and revelations. Joe plans to enrol his son Peter in the army school once he obtains his GCE Ordinary Level and his wife asks if he has discussed the option with Peter. Hear Joe, "There you go, that is why children are spoiled. He has to do what his parents decide for him." Peter who overhears the quarrel tells himself, "No, I will not join the army, if dad refuses to educate me, I will find my own way to become a lawyer." He recalls what his History teacher used to say, "Our future lies in our hands and not with others." "Yes I will struggle for my life," he assures himself.

The rest of the story is not just that of Peter's struggles, but that of his siblings - their trials, their victories. Joe, his wife and an adult world keep on in the background in apparent parallelism. Especially striking is the fact that the characters, who move the story in the main, are young people. Ngozi's profession (a Sister of the Holy Rosary), inadvertently plays into the moral tone admonishing the lives of these young people.

The final message is akin to that of Tatah Mbuy in , "The moral responsibility of the writer in a pluralist society: The case of the Cameroon Anglophone writer," who believes that any human being who is not aware of his moral responsibility, neither deserves to be what he is, nor be where he is." Peter demonstrates such awareness by consciously using his power of choice and choosing the direction of thought that feels good, and it is this that actually makes the tone and quality of his reality and by extension, that of young people specifically and humanity in general.

Ngozi does what Norbert Platt says of the art of putting pen to paper - that it, "...encourages pause for thought, this in turn makes us think more deeply about life, which helps us regain our equilibrium." The range of choices we must make for a fulfilling life are varied, the themes in this novel as myriad as in her first novel, *The Power to Succeed*, but the style and structure here, impress greater mastery of the art.

While a work of art can be treated at any level, this novel can be very appropriate for a secondary school Literature syllabus as it offers relevant perspectives for an approach to interpreting a novel, or prose appreciation in general. It also tickles critical debates on the definition of national Literature; as Ngozi is a Nigerian, but demonstrates a full understanding of Cameroonian realities. Students can easily identify with the issues at the individual, family and socio - political levels; thanks to the acute crafting of characters.

Peter Suh-Nfor Tangyie
Writer, Critic, Theatre/Film Practitioner
Principal, GBHS Bamenda

Introduction

Is it possible to make a difference in your life that no one else has ever made?

What difference will you make as an individual in your life's situations? Have you ever considered yourself a possible obstacle to your future plans?

While some people toil and amass all kinds of knowledge in the world and become the famous scientists, archaeologists, prolific writers, directors, dramatists, musicians, famous businessmen and women, some engage in a life style of political jargon and believe that they can make a difference there. Still, there are some who make a difference in a quiet way and move the world on. The difference you make may lead to negative or positive results and both ways have a price. I feel it is worth exploring the powers you have and discovering the real you. Life is full of surprises. Why get stuck in your narrow world? Life around you might be ignorant but you have the potential to move to a better understanding.

This story portrays and affirms the uniqueness of each person in society and especially in a family set-up: how one moves on in life amidst all the difficulties that life presents. Life is beautiful if you are able to challenge what you can and accept what you cannot change. The difference you can make is within you if you wish to do it.

Society is corrupt, people say. What is society? If people in the society change, society will definitely be renewed. How could you make a change in your own way no matter how small? You can't plan life's perfect moments, but you can give things a nudge in the right direction. It is worth taking trouble to make your life easy. Sometimes difficult choices lead towards life's dream. And what is your dream?

Often we find truth in the simple life style. It took an army of curious scientists sixteen years and undisclosed millions to think up an experiment they were totally in the fog about, while Isaac Newton needed only a single apple to discover the law of gravity. Do you know that the answer to your future is within you?

1

Squabbles

Peter woke up, screwed his eyes and tiptoed to the door, his effort to escape unnoticed failed as the door slammed suddenly. He quickly raced back to his bed and covered his face with the pillow. Silence prevailed for a while. He got up again determined. The irresistible urge in him forced him to crawl slowly and noiselessly like a tortoise out on a ravenous mission. He turned the handle of the door and waited. There was a sound like a whisper which gradually turned into murmur in the house. The building was close to the main road, so it was difficult to spot where the murmur was coming from. He listened again as he unlocked the main door and opened it a little. The noise seemed to be coming from the direction of his parent's room. He closed the door quickly and listened again. The murmur had turned into a noisy encounter and he could hear his mother's voice as the door of their room opened.

'Joe these are all your children. You cannot choose who to love and educate among your children. They all need to be educated.'

Joe responded angrily,

'I did not refuse that they are my children, but I said they will receive the basic education and then they can find their way like other children. I have decided to train my first daughter and that is that.'

'What will people think about your son, he is our only son? You cannot let people laugh at us.'

'I don't care about what people think or say, however I have planned to enrol him in the army school once he finishes his GCE ordinary level.'

'Army school, have you discussed with him what he would like to do?'

'There you go, that is why children are spoiled. He has to do what his parents decide for him.'

'No, Joe, that doesn't sound right. It is not fair; remember that you chose your own career. More-over, that thinking belongs to an out-dated notion of parental control. It does not suit the present generation.'

'This is why the present generation is like this. We give them guns to shoot us and we wallow in their furies.'

'You amaze me when you think this way.'

'I am not ready to go into these details this morning. I am going to be late for work.'

'What of Peter's school fees? Did you read the letter from the principal on the table? If fees are not paid, he will not be registered for his final examination? He may be sent out for not having paid his fees on Monday.'

'You settle that problem okay.' He moved angrily out of the house and banged the door behind him.

'Joe this is how you pushed me to borrow money to complete Sledge's fees in her final year in the first cycle. Now you cannot tell me that there is no money when you received your salary only last week. I find it hard to really understand why you are doing this to me.' She was almost in tears in soliloquy.

Everywhere was still again. Peter waited until he heard the sound of their father's car turn into the main road and he opened the door again quietly. His room was at the rear of the building. His parents' had the first room that backed the gate as you entered the camp and the door to the room led into the big parlour that separated their parents' room from other rooms. The girls occupied the second room. He had to pass his sisters' and his parents' room before he could make it to the gate.

As he tactfully stuck out his head, he looked sideways and there was no one in view. The morning was cold and windy. It had rained non-stop the previous night. The rain was still dribbling like beads as morning unfolded. It was September, the end of the rainy season, but rain continued to pour forbidding the coming of dry weather. He could hear the chirping birds hopping to and fro on the tree-branches, beckoning him to take a leap. He was jealously enthralled by the freedom of those innocent creatures. They do not have to pretend or avoid being caught by any one. They moved freely in search of food and shelter. He wished and longed for such freedom as he reflected on the uproar between his parents that morning. However, he planned how to smuggle himself out of the house without being caught by his eldest sister but then his mind was distracted by his parent's argument. He assured himself aloud.

'No, I will not join the army. If dad refuses to educate me I will find my own way to become a lawyer.' He recalled what his history teacher used to say:

'Our future lies in our hands and not with others.' 'Yes, I will struggle for my life,' he assured himself.

He hurried through the corridor and made a quick dash like lightening to the gate. He unlocked the small entrance gate hastily, but noiselessly and dashed out. It was a red iron gate with a small side entrance. He stood behind the trees outside the gate. He smiled and thanked his lucky stars for his great escape.

He forgot about his parents' quarrel and concentrated on his search.

His eyes moved fast around the trees. His hands went into action. The fruits had been blown down by the wind the previous night. Other children seemed not to have come yet. Luck was on his side. It was a matter of first come, have the best. He took out the small bag from his pocket to put the fruits as he selected them. The cold seemed to penetrate into every fibre of his body. He realized that in his haste, he had forgotten to put on his pullover. But since he who gathers ant-infested maggots must be prepared for the visit of lizards, he ran across the small footpath into the orchard. The cold could not prevent him from racing from one fruit tree to the other. These mangoes and apples kept hunger away from him during the school break especially as he was often not provided with break money or anything to eat.

He was not surprised that lots of old fruit trees were blown down by the gales last night. It was windy. He shivered a little as the cold continued to lay its wicked hand on him.

His thoughts flashed back to what he was supposed to be doing in the house. He was not sure whether he wanted to join in the cleaning activities that went on in the house that Saturday morning. The duties were shared by their mother and those of them who were not cooking had to clean and tidy. Invariably, his duty was to sweep the surroundings of the compound. Normally his eldest sister, Yvonne, would shout his name to come out if he stayed in bed, but that day was exceptionally different. He vividly pictured the face of his sister when she would discover his sudden disappearance. He was consoled that a gift of fruits would calm her anger and squelchy appetite. Then his thoughts deviated and he sighed:

'At the age of fifteen, I am still depending on these apples and mango fruits as my only hope to fight hunger during

4

break at school, and I cannot even go freely to pick them because Yvonne would prefer that I do my house duties. Well I have to provide for myself since my parents cannot give me any money for break.' These fruits are really a God's send,' he smiled.

But then he wondered if their mum would be able to provide his fees that he had overheard them arguing about.

As he searched carefully for the fruits, he was drawn by familiar voices from a distance. His curiosity drove him to the main entrance to the camp and he saw three of his friends, Ngong, Ndi and Ambe coming from the direction of the school. He wondered where they were coming from at that hour of the morning. They spoke in loud voices. It was like a vague meaningless noise in a distance. Then he found himself straining his ears to listen to what they were saying as they drew closer. They were talking and chattering like birds on their first flight out. None of them seemed to be listening to what the other was saying. As they came nearer, he hid his bag of fruits behind one of the old mango trees, called and joined them.

Ngong was trying to monopolize the argument. He was a year older than Peter but almost the same age with Ndi. Ambe was the youngest of the four, just a month younger than Peter. Ngong was galloping over his speech like a parrot in very high speed or like a jet plane. Normally, he was a fast speaker. However, he heard him say:

'I will be the greatest millionaire in my town by hook or by crook. Look at John, he went on, he has built two houses in Eklewindi and he is planning to purchase a four wheel drive car. He travels to America, England, France and Canada at will.'

'Hey boy, you have to be careful, to play hooky or to be a hooligan will not pay you in the end. You have a different destiny from John. John is born with a silver spoon in his mouth while you, Ngong, are from a pauper family background. You are no body, and you are too young to compare yourself with John,' Ndi intercepted him.

'You must be blind not to see the writing on the wall,' Ngong continued, oblivious of what Ndi had said. 'Do you not know that John's father is one of the ministers in Mesong-mesala? He often shifts all the contracts to his son who has no education and cannot think properly.'

Then Ambe came in, in his usual style, slow and steady. He told them how his father had tried to make connections with the powers that be.

'You know what, in the next coming election my father will be appointed as one of the Ministers and I, Ambe, will be a Minister's son. Ha ha ha. I can imagine myself

being conveyed to school in a land cruiser car or some other elegant vehicle, and all my classmates will look up to me with respect as a Minister's son' with a long stress on the word 'Minister' 'as I alighted from the vehicle.' He made a few funny clumsy steps to demonstrate how he would alight from the car and walk leisurely to the classroom. 'The teacher will treat me with great respect as a minister's son.'

Ngong could hardly allow Ambe to finish the last word before he jumped in.

'Did you not hear that the Prime Minister was a very close friend of the President? They grew up together, so the President had to make space for him in his cabinet. If you observed well, you would have noticed that the important posts in the government were all given to people from the same tribe or family. You must know somebody to be there. Education or qualification does not really matter so long as you have Abraham as your father. Those of us who do not

6

have any godfather must find a way to get in or rot in our hopeless dreams.' Then he turned and commented:

'Peter, you are lucky because your father is in the army. At least he would always bring you the surplus of their things.'

Peter reprimanded Ngong,

'Ngong you are building castles in the air. It is not proper to condone evil because corruption will one day erupt and catch up with you and land you in jail.'

'In jail,' Ngong laughed, 'you can never go to jail once money is talking, and that is why I want to get that money.'

'I would like to be educated and fight my way up the ladder,' Peter said.

'Peter, you are from a different class, your father can afford to bring you up so you do not understand what I am talking about,' Ngong intercepted Peter.

'Ngong, don't talk to me like that, what do you know about politics? You don't allow others to offer their suggestions,' Peter observed.

'Peter you are a fool. What suggestion can you make eh, tell me. Do you think that you know everything ....'

As they talked, they heard the sound of a cyclist coming. It was the type of sound that accompanied the Ministers or Governors on their trips. 'The President must be going somewhere or their spies are out on one of their raids,' Ngong thought; then he gave a loud shout and said breathlessly:

'We are doomed; they must have heard us.'

With lightning speed and without looking back, Ngong took to his heels in one direction and the other two fled in different directions. Peter stood where he was, fixed to the ground. Something held him from running. He was an inquisitive fellow who wanted to see before he acted. He could not understand why they were running.

Then he looked behind. He saw no one but felt the gentle breeze swaying the trees to and fro. The cyclist and his entourage had gone. The silence of the moment engulfed him. The rain had ceased. He went in search of his friends.

He saw Ngong caged inside a hole. He could not get himself out and Peter helped him and assured him of his safety. They went in search of the others. They saw Ambe hiding at the back of an abandoned vehicle shivering with fear and clinging to the vehicle as if it was his only saviour. Ndi fell as he was running and hurt his left leg but fear would not allow him to cry out. He came out pretending not to limp. He had to play the strongman.

When they had come together again, there was an uncomfortable silence. Then Peter spoke.

'Why were you on the run? I see no reason why a mere cyclist should provoke such fear in you. Friends, remember what we read in Julius Caesar that a villain dies many times before his actual death. You cannot allow mundane things to make you behave like frightened rats.'

They sighed ominously and then Ndi said:

'You know the toad does not run during the day for nothing. You know it could have been the Minister you were talking about that zoomed along and you know that these people have a secret way of listening, even to the things that are said in a whisper. They have magnetic ears. We could have landed in jail and …'

Peter interrupted him,

'My friend, you are a coward, if what Ngong said about the Minister were true, why shiver like a little child? The time has come for us to stand up and face the reality in our society and I feel that the injustice and corruption we talk about lies in us.'

They all hailed abuses at him. 'Oh Peter, I would not like to lose my family,' retorted Ambe. 'There is a saying that if a child starts to find what killed his father at an early stage, that child will not be alive to discover it. Did you not hear what happened to one of the politicians who spoke out against the government in Furawa?'

The three friends joined together against Peter, but he blurted out.

'The problem in this country is that nobody cares to do anything either because of fear and ignorance or because we have a lot of food and drink, so we are comfortable with our debased situation. You need to make a change in the way you think and see things. Your life should not depend on what people do, say, or think. As for me, I will not develop a long neck or a laisser-faire attitude because some people want to reap what they did not sow'

Ngong retorted, 'Peter, your father takes bribes, he is in the army. He is already part of the corrupt system. Corruption is already in your blood. So do not pretend to be innocent of what is happening in the country. Everybody knows.'

Peter responded firmly,

'Even if my father is part of that system, I would not conform to the corrupt system. I would rather fight corruption with conviction and an objective mind. With God on my side, I will do things differently.'

They all jeered at him and said, 'God, as if you go to church, Bishop Pius the thirtieth,' and laughed sonorously.

Peter knew that to argue with his fickle-minded friends would be a waste of time, so he let them blather and walked away.

9

He recalled what happened on their way back from school on a day an argument broke out about political unrest in the country. Some of his friends argued that Mfoum and Nanga-Eboko people were senseless and fickle- minded to join the Sala who made them lose their identity, their culture and their language and became slaves in their own land. Some said that it was wise to follow the people who could provide for your needs, give you employment and the opportunity to go abroad; that the Nki'mbang only know how to speak grammar and force you to work like drudges and demand taxes on virtually every item, so that in the end, you were left penniless and helpless.

The supporters of the Mesong-Mesala group went on to blame the people of -Furawa and Eklewindi who followed the Nki'mbang who robbed them of their brotherly love and unity. They ended up being neither Cameroonians nor Nki'mbang but people with no identity.

The Eklewindi and Furawa supporters retorted that the Sala are a devil in disguise. They offer us a job in exchange for our freedom. Indirectly, we become their slaves though we claim to have gained independence.

The argument went on and on with nobody listening to the other.

Peter kept quiet in his usual way and listened. The argument became so intense that they were at the verge of quarrelling. Peter warned them to stop such a dangerous argument.

Ambe directed the question at him as if he was waiting for the opportunity to face him, 'Peter, where do you belong? You are neither here nor there, always playing the Judas.'

Peter retorted, 'I will not support any of you because you have no facts. Besides, you are not sharing your views, but you are blowing off steam at one another. It's an ill wind that blows nobody any good. That is not what we need now in the country. We need to come together as one and think how we can put our thoughts and our country together especially us, the future generation.'

'Yes, we need development,' Ndi added.

'But you cannot climb a steep hill in third gear or else you are heading for a crash,' said Peter. Peter used the opportunity to explain the havoc which insensitivity had caused in the government.

'Yes, but how can development come to Cameroon when our best brains and talented people are all in America, Europe, Canada and other foreign countries receiving fat and exorbitant salaries, consequently, marrying Sala women? Our problem lies within us. Yes, development and change can only come within us. However, when we seek it elsewhere, it could sweep us off our feet and we end up being slaves in other people's land and strangers in our own land. Our freedom and rights are in jeopardy because we only go out to criticize what is happening rather than bringing in something new to build up. In our foolishness we sell our land and ourselves to the Sala and Nki'Mbang people and turn round to complain about their being paranoid. Now we are neither Cameroonians, Sala nor Nki'Mbang. We are like bats that do not belong anywhere, and only fly at night. Things fall apart and there is no centre to bring us together.'

Nobody responded. Peter continued,

Here in our country, the Cameroonians are not one, though; we claim to be one nation. We better look for the black goat amongst us.'

'Mind what you say. It is said that even walls can hear a whisper in hideouts. I would not like to lose my family and my life.' Ambe retorted.

'It is true,' Ndi came in, many people have lost their lives because of such utterances and some have fled the country for safety and the families they left behind were punished.'

Peter told them that such thoughts and rumours would not help them to reason like free citizens.

'When you live in fear of what people would do or say, you can never grow or reason like a real human being. You can never stand up to fight for your right and freedom.' He however reminded them that their argument gave a distorted and highly tendentious view of the political situation in the country.

Ngong who was among those in the group who had been boiling with anger got up, stood in front of Peter and addressed him impulsively.

'Why don't you reserve that preaching for your father who also contributed to the mess we are in? He is a soldier. He should have fought for our independence.' Peter kept quiet and Ngong went on to provoke him,

'Even the so-called army people could not defend the country against the numerous armed robbers in the country; they only collect 500 francs from drivers on the road , such a hungry pack of fools,' he sneered.

As he went on and on, the other boys cajoled Peter to teach that small boy a lesson, but Peter remembered what his mother told him one day.

It was the day he was insulted at school by one of the pupils that he slapped and he fainted. The teacher was not in the class at the time. He was rushed to the hospital. When he came back his mother told him never to react or touch anybody especially when he was angry and not in control of his feelings.

'Insults will never kill you,' she had told him.

Peter told Ngong that two people could not be mad at the same time and walked away. He believed that he must work hard to do things not because others forced him to do them. One must be ready to work hard to make the difference one would love to see in the world.

The sun had risen dispelling the moody morning. Peter moved back to the orchid, picked his bag of fruits and went back to the house. He overheard his eldest sister, Yvonne, humming in the kitchen as she went about her daily chores. He was not sure where the rest of the family was. He went in search of his mother.

2

The Family Situation

'Mum it seems to me that dad is too passionate about his profession. I don't want to be a military man,' Peter began as soon as his mother came in view. Mary beckoned him to sit beside her.

'You see my son, your dad was not happy that you will not like to toe the line of his profession and you prefer something else,' Mary began. 'When Joe was your age, he had refused to continue his advanced studies, and nobody had bothered him till one day he came and declared that he wanted to join the police force. He became a police officer at the age of twenty and later joined the army. He had worked in different parts of the country. And he believed that it is the best career for any young man in this country.'

'Yes as a little boy I saw him as a proud man who also loved his profession.'

'You are right, your father blended his work with care and love for his children in the early stages of our marriage, but...' Peter interrupted.

' Mum I remember when I was seven; I used to walk with him hand in hand. I felt proud too. I would look up at my father's face and think, 'He is the most handsome man in the world.'

Mary laughs and affirms, 'He is a handsome man.'

'On Sundays, dad would take me out for mass while the girls would go with you. We often sat in the middle row and wore squeaky-clean shoes. At the offertory, he would pass me

25 francs, and I recalled longing to keep it as I reluctantly dropped it into the box.' They laughed.

'So you were able to control your urge and let the money go, good boy.'

'Mum it was weird because I did not understand how I could give money away while I needed it for my sweets in the school.'

'But it was meant for God and not for your sweets.'

'I did not understand. You know how dad behaved then, he did not explain to me why I should offer the money to priests who looked healthier and richer than us. Now dad hardly mentions or goes to church.'

'He works on Sundays and moves a lot.'

'Mum I cannot join the police force or army.'

'Why not?'

'It makes us move from place to place where ever dad is transferred we keep changing schools and leaving our friends behind. It is not easy to make new friends all the time. Sledge said that she did not enjoy her school days because of transfers. I can see her point because it is affecting me.'

'But it is the nature of his work.'

'Why should he force me to live his kind of life?'

'Is that your reason for not accepting that career?'

'I do not like that job because it makes my father violent even at home. I feel sad when he beats us and you as well. He drinks a lot.'

Mary felt sad that her children had discovered all these things about their father. She never got used to that movement from one place to another, but in her quiet way she never complained. She knew the family would disintegrate if she was not close to Joe.

Peter recalled how his father used to visit drinking places as soon as he received his salary 'to wash his mouth with

16

coloured water' as he used to call beer and strong drinks. Then he would come home and beat his mother. That usually happened whenever he received his salary at the end of the month. When the neighbours ran in to help, their mother would dismiss them with a sentence: 'You are not invited,' and they would turn away disappointed.

Peter often wondered why she did not want outsiders to know what was going on in the house. He was not happy with his father's attitude but he was too young to intervene. He prayed that one day he would be old enough to challenge their father.

'Papa becomes violent whenever he gets drunk. Then he turns dowdy when he becomes sober. I think his profession as an army man must have contributed to his bohemian behaviour and I hate that profession.'

'Your father is stuck in it. It is not an enchanting attitude.'

'But mum why prevent people from coming in to help when dad hits you?

'There is no family without problems so let one carry one's own cross. All the pots that have gone through the charcoal fire must have traces of black no matter how well you wash them. There is no point washing your dirty linen in public.'

Their mother's attitude moulded their lives as children. They never told their story to anyone, but secretly shared it among themselves. If any of them hurt the other, they would only talk to the person concerned. They endured whatever correction they got from their parents without complaining or sharing it with outsiders. People knew that their father often beat their mother but they had no evidence because they were never let in.

On that Monday morning, the children went to school. Mary managed to clear Peter's fees and he was enrolled for his GCE examination. Yvonne's fees had been paid two weeks after the term resumed. Sledge who had finished her GCE the year before went to Nanga-Eboko and Mesong-Mesala in search of a job as their father refused to pay for her education to do Advanced Level. Kelly was in her third level in the secondary school.

A month later was the last day of the term. The morning was very busy. It was Peter's final year in the first cycle of secondary education. They had just finished writing their GCE Examination. Other students in classes one to four had gone home one week before the GCE began. Some of the students abandoned their books in class due to unfounded excitement. Others thought that they had come to the end of the road in education because it looked interesting and exciting to be moving out of school. It was the last day mates would see one another for a long time.

Uncertainty loomed in the air as the students packed their things. Some students were happy because they were sure to pass, while others were neither happy nor sad because they were not sure what result they would get. The final year students were busy exchanging addresses and discussing what they would do when they leave school. The whole atmosphere was noisy like an open market square.

Peter had hoped that the school would close earlier that day but they kept on cleaning the school compound till 11 a.m. He would miss his friends. Some of his friends were going to continue their higher education abroad.

His thoughts flashed to his friends. Ndi was to leave the country as soon as he dropped his pen; a golden plate had been placed on his lap. Ambe would go for medical training in Canada. Cyprian would join his uncle in Sala. Irene, his girlfriend, was going to continue her professional training as a nurse in Nki'Mbang. Ngong said he would stay in the country

18

because he wanted to climb the political ladder. He was not interested in education. He believed strongly that his connections would help him in his political aspirations without education. Moses and a handful of others were not sure of what they would do.

Peter's mind zoomed back home. His thoughts stumbled on what his father had planned already. His father had told him one day that he would like him to join the armed forces, but he had not said anything after that or made any efforts to enrol him. Peter did not like the profession either. He would love to further his education at the university and study law. He had once dreamt that he saw himself on a very high tree filled with fruits and from where he fed everyone who could not climb the tree. The opportunity to further his education was very slim and in fact far-fetched.

He wondered if his mother would continue to support him with her meagre earnings. She was trained to be a government teacher but their batch was so unfortunate that the government had no more vacancies in the schools located in town. They were not assigned to any school. All the government schools in urban areas were over-staffed. Nobody wanted to go to the rural areas to teach. The village schools were not equipped like the urban schools and the roads were absolutely horrible. She looked for a job for almost two years. Eventually, she was employed in one of the private schools in Town. The whole family depended on her little salary most of the time. In addition to her teaching, she had to work on the farm and do '*buy am sell am*' to make ends meet.

His father, Joe, did not pay all the fees despite the fact that he earned a handsome salary. He spent his money on what he described as important issues. Joe however, was not interested in the education of his children but he promised to educate Yvonne his first daughter to any level.

The house was empty when Peter arrived home. Their mother and Kelly were out on the farm. Joe had travelled to Yaoundé. Sledge had gone in search of a job and Yvonne was not back from school. His worries could not be shared with anyone.

It was clear to him that he would fend for himself.

When Mary came back from the farm Peter related to her how the school ended and also about his other friends who had planned to further their education. Mary was sad because she knew that her husband wanted Peter to join his profession. She had asked Peter what he would like to do. Peter told her that he would like to continue his advanced level education and then go to university to study law. She wanted their son to be educated but could not understand why her husband was so unconcerned about his future. She saw her past life foreboding the happiness of her son.

Mr Joe came back two days later; he reopened the idea of enrolling Peter in the army school. Peter told him exactly what he told his mother about studying law. Mr Joe laughed and said, 'My son will never do a thing like that because it is a dishonest profession.'

'What is dishonest about being a lawyer?' Mary asked.

He laughed again, 'Do you not know that lawyers are the trained thieves we have in this country? Their dubious attitude is indubitable. They not only steal with deceitful words but with their nibble pointed pens. They are not honest people. They are like the rats that must cajole and blow at their victims. They are all scapegoats.'

Peter was taken aback by his father's utterances. Peter remembered what one of his friends had said about the army in one of their hot arguments.

'Even the so-called army people cannot defend the country against the numerous armed robbers in the country; they only collect 500 francs from the drivers on the roads.'

And here was their father condemning others. It was true that one could not see one's back no matter how one turned. It was the pot calling the kettle black.

'There is no profession that is not corrupt in the world today,' Mary came in, 'but a lot depends on the individuals who are in those professions. If they have a clean mind and heart, they can make a difference. You can only make a change within you when you desire it. And the change you make within can challenge the whole world.'

Joe responded sharply. 'I do not believe in that philosophy of life.' and he waved his hands and continued. 'Peter, if you insist on being a lawyer, then you will find a way to educate yourself, but if you are ready to be trained as an army officer, I will enrol you the following week.'

'It is not right to force a child to accept a profession that he will not like. It is against the ethics of human freedom.' Mary pleaded with her husband.

'Please do not be too hard on our son. I know you can educate him if you want.'

'Well, he can look for a job and together with you become a lawyer or whatever he likes, but you should not depend on me for any financial support.' He finished and walked away.

Peter knew that when their father was not in support of anything it was like pouring water on a stone. Peter decided to support himself. Jobs were difficult to find in that part of the country. You could only get a job as a teacher or nurse if you were trained. The next option was to either be a trader or self-employed doing things like hairdressing or sewing or to be a craftsman apprentice in carpentry or motor repairs or to work as a steward in the Brasseries Company. Peter could hardly get any job with just G.C.E. Ordinary Level results.

He searched for jobs at various construction sites for months without any luck.

One fateful morning, a neighbour offered him work in his farm. He did the work very well and the man invited him for a second day. After one week, the work ended. He did odd jobs here and there and earned little money. There were days when he was not paid after work, but he kept working all the same. Peter wore the same pair of trousers every day and only had one meal a day usually gateau or dry bread, except he visited his mother at the school, and she bought a meal for him.

Peter decided to try his luck elsewhere and went down to Mpongo. He got a job in one of the building construction sites in Mpongo. The work was never steady. Worse still they were not paid the little they were supposed to earn.

Two months had elapsed and they had not been paid. He thought of abandoning the job.

He had decided to discontinue and to inform the site manager the next morning when the clock turned against him.

On that morning, Peter came and discovered that the workers were all standing and staring at the place.

'Why are you all standing here like logs of wood?' He expected his co- workers to respond cheerfully as usual but no one spoke. Peter saw the look of worry on their faces and then asked one of them called Okon what happened.

'There is a case of theft at the site. Someone had made away with some of the building materials: 20 bags of Cement, packets of nails, five shovels and a roll of 2.5mm binding-wire were missing from the store.'

'Eh, did they ask the store keeper?'

'The storekeeper feigned surprise and worry too. So we are suspects and the manager has sent for the Police to come and arrest us.'

They were interrogated, but no one accepted blame for or could give an account of the missing items. The family of other boys bailed them after two weeks. Peter remained in detention for another week before Mr Joe could come down to bail him. Initially Mr Joe refused to bail him.

'I cannot bail a thief, let him bear the consequence.'

'Our son is not a thief. He has never stolen before. Why must you listen to the gossip?'

'And why must he engage in the site filled with thieves if he is not one.'

'Joe please do not judge it like that. This circumstance is beyond his power. How do you expect to know what would happen in the site? Please go down and bail him.'

His wife pleaded till he went to Mpongo.

Peter's experiences behind the bar were very unpleasant. He was forced to serve an old, rich but brutal fellow occupant who was a murderer and had been there for 10 years. He was made to answer him 'Sir' as if he was his father. Worst still, he could not stomach the filthy environment he found himself in. In fact his room was stinking and he remained at the corridor most of the time except when he was shouted upon to get inside his cell. They were fed once a day and the food was better fit for the pigs rather than humans. He had made do with the food because there was nobody to bring food for him.

When Peter came out from jail, his father spoke angrily to him,

'I have asked you to join my profession but you adamantly refused. I will not appear again if you get yourself into another mess.'

Peter left that place and went to another part of the town to look for a job. It was difficult to get a job on another site for the news of the theft had gone round like wild fire in all directions.

He tried to engage himself in a car wash since some of the people that came to wash their cars did not stay in Mpongo. There were many boys doing the same job. There were days he could not wash even one car. He wallowed his way from cocoa plantation to plantain plantation, but the work was seasonal. He was never sure what each day would bring.

His quest for education continued to fan his strength. He hoped that out of darkness light would one day shine. The power within kept him in constant hope.

One day a friend informed him that he could register for the Advanced Level Examination as an external candidate. He took the bull by the horns and registered. He divided his time between his petty jobs and his studies. He was sad about his father's behaviour and exclaimed one day:

'I cannot understand why my father could not transfer the money he would use for my army training for my desired career. I have yet to discover why he dislikes me.'

Peter decided to visit home and surprisingly found his family in a shamble and devastated state.

3

Family Struggles

The night was dull and dark. It looked like the sky had shot itself completely out. Joe had suddenly begun to return late from work and gave reasons that there was urgent work to finish. Though one could smell beer on his body. Mary decided not to complain because it often earned her a beating. There had been a big commotion about the night beatings that went on for weeks at home. The straw that broke the camel's back was when Joe received his June salary plus the allowances due to him. He went to the off-license as he used to do whenever he received his salary and drank as many bottles of beer as his stomach could accommodate. In his fury, he declared surplus for all the people present in the drinking place. The rest of the money had either been lost on his way back or was stolen. He came home very late at night shouting at the top of his voice. They had thought that he would not come back that night. He demanded his food. Yvonne ran to the kitchen to warm the food and the next thing she heard amidst shouting was a cry that sounded so terrible. Yvonne heard her father shouting and arguing with her mum.

'Who removed the money I kept in my left pocket?'

'But you have just come and you have not removed your clothes, so how can someone have removed the money?' Mary asked.

'You think I am drunk or have lost my senses. I know I put my money in this pocket till I entered this house.' He touched the pocket, Where is it?'

25

'That sounds strange. I had no idea you came back with money. You are the one who woke me up from sleep with your shouting.'

'Oh you slept without your husband and I have to be questioned for waking up my own wife. May be you are having somebody there with you. And may I ask who the dubious man is?'

'Joe what are you insinuating? Please let me go and see if your food is ready. It is too late for us to begin quarrelling.'

As Mary moved to the door, Joe blocked the way and pushed her back.

'You think I am out of my mind. I asked you two questions which you have not answered and you think you can run away from them.' He started beating his wife.

'Joe stop beating me. I do not have your money and as you can see there is no man in the house.'

'Oh! Oh so I am not man enough to be in the house. Yeah, there is no man in the house, tell me more.'

'Please I am not ready for this uproar. You know I only responded to your question.'

'What is my question? Tell me what my question is, useless woman!'

Mary could not respond to him at that stage. He beat her till she became unconscious. She was beaten within an inch of her life. Mary was rushed to the hospital and from there she returned to her parent's house for complete recovery. Kelly went with her. Yvonne remained with their father.

Peter, oblivious of what had happened at home travelled the whole night on a bus from Mpongo to Furawa to see his parents during the weekend. Usually the night bus left at nine o'clock in the evening and arrived at Furawa in the early hours of the morning. The road from South-west to Furawa was not smooth and there were plenty of bends. The drivers

26

were used to the dangerous corners but they had to drive carefully as there were dark spots. While people enjoyed their sleep in the bus, the driver moved on till he stopped at the eating arena. Those sleeping and snoring were woken up by others so that they could refill their stomachs. People were very friendly and cared for one another in the bus; it was part of the African warmth and understanding that they behaved like brothers and sisters especially when they were away from their homes.

There were always varieties of food and things to buy at the rest stop: roasted and fried plantains, roasted fish and chickens, potatoes and cocoyams, and a host of other foods. The foods were always delicious, tempting and made one salivate. Peter bought his roasted plantains, fish and drink and went back to his seat to enjoy. He bought a bottle of water to wash the food down. There were assorted drinks; different kinds of soft drinks ranging from coke, Fanta, sprite, 7up and others. Cokes and sprites were filled in 1.5cl big plastic bottles, and fruit juice like oranges or mango juice in small cans of 30cl. Fruits like mango, pawpaw, oranges, apples, pears and avocados, were available as well.

People of course do not smoke inside the vehicles, but those who needed to smoke ran out as soon as the bus stopped to do their business before the bus moved on again. The break normally lasted thirty minutes before the journey continued.

When Peter arrived home in the early hours of the morning, his family was still asleep. He knocked hard at the gate before he could be heard. Yvonne got up and inquired about the caller. It was part of the culture to know who the caller was before responding or opening the door.

Before Peter could ask about anyone, Yvonne narrated to him what had happened a few weeks ago. Peter was not surprised about the beating but he was taken aback that their mum had to go to her parents. He knew their mother was a patient woman and always forgave their father whenever the beatings took place. Peter thought that whatever made her leave home must have been serious.

The next day Yvonne accompanied Peter to see their mother. They had planned to beg her to come back home for their sake. When they arrived, Kelly told them that their mother had been admitted in hospital again. She was there with Pat, her mother. Peter hurried back and informed their father.

Mr Joe was frightened and followed him immediately. He was worried to the bones because he was not sure if she were still alive. Despite all the difficulties, the children knew their father loved their mother dearly. When they arrived at the hospital, Mary was asleep and the doctor had warned that she should not be disturbed. Mr Joe waited outside the ward.

As they waited, Peter's thoughts travelled around.

'Why do people do things to upset the peace in the family?'

He realized that any man who indulged in drinking and smoking would always behave like their father.

He remembered Ambe's story about how his father was rescued from the gutter. He was lucky that the gutter had been empty; he might have drowned in the rain before being rescued. He also recounted how a teacher was dismissed because he drank to intoxication during the class period and played jazz in the classroom. He could still hear the uproar in his class before the principal rescued the situation.

He wished he could talk to their father but he knew the time was not yet ripe to challenge him.

He reflected on the gossip he had heard, that many people in this country love drink more than food and that the world sees Cameroonians as the third highest consumers of alcohol. He wondered which countries were first and second. This brought a smile to his face; at least his country was not among the first two.

He wondered if that analysis was true. He would read more books to see what happened in other countries. He hoped he would become a literary scholar and help his country. He was interrupted by the banging of the door as the nurse came out to the corridor to inform their dad that their mum was awake.

When Mary woke up, she was not sure where she was. Her mother was very happy that she woke up. The nurse on duty was relieved and happy that she had revived because she was very ill. Joe came in and stood at a distance. Mary looked in his direction and he was encouraged to come nearer. Mary's mother refused to talk with Joe. She ignored his greeting. She was nursing her anger and pain.

Joe asked the children to return to the house and he stayed with their mum in the hospital. Their mother recovered faster than the doctor had anticipated.

In the hospital Joe earnestly asked his wife to forgive him. When she got well, they had planned to go together and beg Mary's parents to forgive him and allow them to go back to their home.

Mary looked through the window and saw her father rushing to the hospital. It was unusual for her father to walk in that fast pace. Mary's mother ran to meet him and they went straight to the doctor. Mary sat up on the bed and waited.

'Doctor I want to know the condition of my daughter's health,' Paul asked.

'She is responding well. She may be discharged either today or tomorrow,' the doctor told him.

'Paul, I have to take my daughter back home as soon as she is discharged,' Mary's Mother burst out.

Paul came to Mary's bed. He barely responded to Joe's greeting and there was no conversation.

'I have come to take you to my house.'

'I will bring her home when she is discharged Sir,' came in Joe.

'That is beside the point,' responded Paul. 'I just need to take my daughter home before you kill her.' Mary's parents were not ready for feigned repentance or unfounded forgiveness. They just needed to take their daughter home.

Mary's mother blurted out,

'My husband had never beaten me for the sixty years of our marriage. I cannot understand how an educated and intelligent man like you should be pounding my daughter as if she is not a human being with flesh and blood or you think that perhaps she has no body to defend her.

However, Joe followed like a prodigal son to see his wife home when she was discharged. Joe's in-laws told him to go home and reconsider whether he wanted to continue living with their daughter.

It was a moment of sadness for the family. Joe went home with Peter and Yvonne while Kelly remained with their mother.

Joe began to lose appetite and became moody. The children were handicapped and sad too. Peter could not go back to his job, but went every week to plead with his grandfather. Joe continued his work but did not return home often. When he eventually came back he would not eat but only drink. The situation was deteriorating and Yvonne feared that one day he might beat her because of how he shouted at her at every slightest thing.

Mary would have loved to go back to her husband but her parents had told her that if she tried to disobey them, they would never listen to her again and would turn their backs on her.

'That man has to learn a lesson for once. Your mother and I had heard a lot about how he used to beat you almost every month. We did not bring you up to be killed by him. If you disobey us, you know what will happen,' Paul warned.

'Mary, my daughter, you cannot forgive him like that. It does not work that way. He must either apologise or you stay with us.'

'Mama I am worried about my children,' said Mary.

'Do not bother; he can take care of them,' Pat responded.

Three months had elapsed and Joe waited impatiently for Mary to turn up but nothing happened. He went and consulted his family. They agreed to visit their in-laws with five bottles of wine and ten cartons of beer to plead. It was Joe's uncle who spoke.

'Our in-laws, we came with these drinks to say that we have wronged your daughter, our wife and your entire household,' began Kingsly. 'My brother has made a mistake by laying hands on your precious daughter and our good wife. There is a saying that if there is no bad behaviour, there will be nothing to apologize for. That does not mean to say we must commit crimes to create reasons for forgiveness. I have discussed with my brother and he has promised it will not happen again. We love our wife and we would like to have her back.'

And Joe presented the drinks.

'It is not bravery for a man to beat his wife,' his in- laws told Joe. 'That my daughter survived the last beating was a miracle. The people who took her to the hospital thought she was dead. How have I wronged you by allowing you to get married to my daughter?'

'You did nothing wrong, replied Kingsly. It is our human frailty.'

'I am not sure whether Joe has reflected enough on how he will treat my daughter in the future. I would like to hear from him.'

Joe stood up, cleared his throat and opened his mouth but no words came out. He stood for quite a while and the atmosphere was quiet and a bit tense. At last he gathered courage and spoke in an emotional and shaky voice.

'I am ashamed of myself to have gathered this crowd here because of my insolent behaviour. I am aware of my behaviour's dangerous and destructive effect on my family and my life, and yet it is difficult for me to stop. I promise to do my best. I love my wife. I would have come earlier but … he could no longer speak and lowered his head.

'Joe, you have to promise me that you will never beat Mary again. You are a strong man. The work of any man is to protect his family and not to hurry them to their graves. I would not like you to create this type of nasty opportunity for me to intervene again between you and my daughter.'

'I promise not to touch her again.'

'I did not say not to touch her, she is your wife, but not to beat her,' people smiled at the sense of humour and silence reigned again.

Mary's father beckoned his wife to call Mary to ascertain if she was ready to go back with Joe. Mary came out and went and held her husband. It was a moment of reunion.

Joe took his wife back home. Children love their parents despite their short comings. Peter had such firm belief in the bright side of the future. Before he went back to Mpongo he told his mother to be patient with their father till the time when he would be able to make a difference in their life. Mary had laughed at her son's concern about her and assured him that she would wait till he performed wonders.

4

Yvonne's Situation

While their mother was away, Yvonne had been dating and running around with a boy who had no job or plan for his future. Her studies were neglected and the relationship became her focus. She had just turned 21 and felt she could do whatever she liked with her life.

Their father was interested in his first daughter, and had wanted to train her up to University level, but she had what could be described as an average brain for learning. She took seven years instead of five to obtain her GCE O level papers before she was qualified to do the advanced level. She had not been able to pass that level. She wanted to do linguistics at University, but could not get enough papers to apply for the course. The irony of it was that their father loved Yvonne more than any of his children.

She came home one day with a boy and introduced him to her parents as her possible suitor. Joe was very angry and told his daughter off. The boy had no decent job and in fact, he was more of a tout (motor boy) in the car station.

'It is only illiterate girls like you who leave their future unattended to get married to a useless nonentity. Look at your younger sister Sledge, she makes an effort to be somebody in the society but you are preparing yourself for a disaster.' Joe warned her. 'That will not happen in my house, here is not Nki'Mbang or Sala countries where children are left to run wild in the name of freedom. Either you listen to me or you move away and cease to be my child,' he ended with that finality of tone.

'But I love him.' Yvonne responded.

'Where did you get the stamina to say you love him before me? Joe questioned her angrily. 'You cannot even speak correct grammar. So you are the one arranging the marriage. No marriage arranged in this form ever worked. Do you not know that women who have things to offer, pride themselves very highly and men look for them. The days are gone when women sit in the house and take care of babies. Do you hear me? It is because you are preoccupied with that bastard that you cannot learn anything. So forget that idiot and face your studies or you meet your doom.'

However, Yvonne ignored her father's threats and continued dating her boyfriend. Her heart had gone with him and she stopped attending school. Their mother also warned her to stop dating the boy, but as the proverb says,

'The flies that would enter the grave with the corpse do not listen to the warning bell of the mourners. Don't let this boy jeopardize your future and the love your father has for you,' her mother had told her.

The irony of the story was that the boy was really jobless. He was also a dropout from the government school in Mesong- Mesala. He had told Yvonne that his parents wanted him to settle down and form his own family. They would be happy to have a grand son and his greatest desire was to get married to Yvonne and have a son. He wanted a child more than a wife. He hoped that when that happened, his uncle in America would send him money. If it was not enough his cousin in United Kingdom would supplement him. He would call them and let them know that he was getting married. Yvonne was very excited and was carried away by the story. She actually believed him and even nursed the hope of

36

travelling to Europe one day to visit his uncle or cousin when they were married.

She gave deaf ears to her parent's advice and went away with him.

Reflecting over the past experiences of her few friends who were not married, but had babies. Yvonne remembered vividly how many of them suffered because they had children out of wedlock. Some were forced to do demeaning labour up to and after giving birth, working in horrid conditions for little or no pay. Some were beaten, others starved, and the majority mistreated by their parents. To the Church they were sinners and forced repentance was their only path to salvation. Most, though, were mere peasant girls who had no good family upbringing and could ill afford to raise a child. Others were girls who had the ill fortune to become pregnant against their boyfriends' wishes. After birth, some of them abandoned their babies in the hospital. Some were taken by their mothers to wean.

Manka's experiences flooded her mind and she was almost overwhelmed by it. She was a victim of unplanned love.

Manka was fifteen years old and a spinster when she became pregnant. Her parents warned her never to abort the baby. The parents and her friends neglected her partly out of shame and partly because Manka refused to name her boyfriend. She was forced to do demeaning labour for little or no pay. She finally gave up the child for adoption to the orphanage.

'That no fit happen for my corner,' she assured herself in pidgin.

Yvonne was consoled by the fact that Ben and his parents would accept the child if it came because they wanted a grandchild. She was sure that her case would be different from those of other girls who brought shame on their families. She was hopeful that if she got pregnant; their father would mellow and accept Ben. She felt that presenting him to her parents was wise so she was different from other girls. Besides, Ben would never abandon her she convinced herself.

She packed her things and went to stay with Ben. Education was forgotten. Within two months she became pregnant. She was happy that she was satisfying Ben. She hoped that he would then introduce her to his parents once she became pregnant but there was no move to take her to his parents. Ben kept on telling her that their marriage would be one in town when she had delivered the baby.

'If you give me a boy pikin, I go make e king for my heart,' he used to say in pidgin and they would laugh. He also spoke French and English, but since Yvonne spoke pidgin often, he joined her at times. Things began to change gradually as Yvonne approached the seventh month of her pregnancy.

Her parents did not talk about Yvonne in the house but their mother was really worried.

Invariably, the news came to Peter as a rumour that his eldest sister has got married. He was upset about it. He was sure that something was wrong and wondered why their mother did not tell him. He decided to go home during the weekend to find out the truth. He boarded the night bus to Furawa and arrived on a Saturday morning. He met their mother in the house. The father had travelled to Maroua. Mary had no clue as to the whereabouts of Yvonne. They had neither seen nor heard from her since she left home.

'Yvonne left the house nearly a year ago to an unknown destination,' she explained. 'I have tried to find out where she is but have not succeeded. Some of her friends said that they used to see her at times in the commercial avenue but they did not know where she was staying. Your father swore that he would never look for her and that she would skin her alive if he ever set his eyes on her. Peter, 'I am really tired,' she sighed. 'I did not tell you because she ran away from home. It is my fault entirely.'

Peter knew one of Yvonne's best friends. He went to see her. She had a hair salon shop in the main market. Eileen's hair was palmed and arranged neatly with ribbon at the back. She was about the age of Yvonne and specialized in hair dressing and beauty salon. She gave him the address and also told him that since she gave birth a few months ago, she had neither seen her or her boyfriend. They used to come around before then. Peter went in search of the place.

He searched for a whole day but could not locate the place. The houses were disorganized and difficult to locate as some places barely had footpaths almost invisible to a stranger. As his heart stumbled in his chest, he stepped around a store in a corner and asked the lady to help him with the numbering of the houses in the area.

'There was no house number,' the woman told him.

The houses were not really numbered in that quarter. People just build at the available space. He inquired about any new couples that must have been living around there. She told him that she was not aware of any new couple around but, there was a boy who used to stay with his girlfriend at the corner there. She pointed at the house but she had no hint of their way about for months. She was not sure if they had gone away.

Peter went to the house and knocked at the locked door. There was no answer. He tried again and peeped through the door. There was no word. He looked around the compound. There was no compound. All the spaces were taken up by the building, which was in a very bad shape. The surrounding looks filthy and out of human habitation. Empty tins of milk, sardine, tomato and other containers were littered round the place.

The air was contaminated with rotten foods and water left inside tins and things. His stomach began to turn. He wondered how anyone could accept to live in a place like that. He moved from there; he had to walk slowly so as to avoid being trapped in the pot holes scattered on the narrow path before he joined the new constructed tarred road.

'No, Yvonne cannot be here,' he told himself and walked away.

He went back to the store he had just passed and unfortunately the lady had locked up the store and left. He regretted not buying biscuits or drink to quench his thirst. He had to walk miles before he could see another store. Then a thought came to him to follow the opposite direction. He was not willing to give up just like that though it was getting late and he was worried that his mother would begin to look for him as well. He had no phone to call home. His fear for the worst kept him going. To his surprise, he found himself where he had started. He discovered that he had been going round and round the village. The village was not that big. Instinctively he went and knocked at the same door and there was no response. He stood and resigned to go home. The weather had changed and it was getting dark. There was no street light. He decided to go home and continue the search the next day.

As he was about to go, he tapped hard at the door again. Then he thought he heard a voice struggling to speak. He called Yvonne many times and was sure that somebody was in the house. He waited for quite a while and there came the cry of a child within the house. He could see that someone was struggling with the handle of the door within. And the door opened. What he saw made him shift back. He could not believe his eyes.

The power to scold or ask questions left him and it was replaced by compassion and immediacy. There was no need to ask questions because it was clear that the mother and child were not just ill, but they were half way to the grave. He helped her to get ready and took her and the child away to the general hospital. They were admitted immediately. Yvonne's blood and urine had to be taken in the ward because she had no strength to go to the laboratory. They gave her drips and injections and she slept. The child had a high fever and cried a lot. Peter stayed with her the whole night till morning when she regained consciousness. She asked where she was. She recognized Peter for the first time and shouted in a low tone.

'Peter how you did you discover where I live and where is my baby?'

'Your baby is safe. You will see him in a moment,' Peter replied.

Peter tried to bring her up to date on what had happened.

'I searched for you all day. I knocked at your door many times and I was about to give up when the child cried. It is difficult to believe that you would be in a house like that. But you are brave to have walked to the hospital with the kind of weak body you have. You were so sick and unconscious that the nurses decided to put the child in a separate bed. The nurses took care of the child all night.'

She kept looking down and tears dripped down from her eyes like a running tap. She allowed them to drop on her lap. Then tearfully she asked Peter again

'Peter how did you find this place? Who told you where I was?'

'Eileen gave me your address and I looked for the number the whole day. I am glad that I discovered where you were. The important thing now is that I am here and you are safe,' Peter consoled.

She started crying aloud.

It was difficult to convince her that they would go home to their parents from the hospital two weeks later when she was discharged though their mother came to see her.

'Papa will never forgive me. I am dead. He warned me against that hooligan but I was blind and foolish to see the hand writing on the wall.

How can I go home?' she wondered dejectedly.

'You will begin by coming with me. We will sort it out; mum would be happy to see you. She has been crying every day for you. She knows that things are not going well for you,' Peter explained.

They left the hospital on Monday morning. Peter took the bill and went home with Yvonne and the child.

Their mother was really relieved and happy to see her. Yvonne was very pale and malnourished. After few days she regained a little bit of strength but was very weak and moody. She wept for days. One night she could not sleep and she went to her mother and cried.

'I am aware that you have not fully recovered,' her mother told her, 'do not hurry to talk.'

'Yes mama but my heart is heavy. I cannot rest unless I share my life and experience with you. I feel sad about my behaviour. Yes, I was foolish to follow that idiot for what I thought was true love.' She narrated her experience with Ben.

Yvonne met Ben at the wedding ceremony of her friend. He was very gentle and soft spoken. He showed her a lot of concern and love and Yvonne thought she had met someone who cared about her and fell in love at first sight. They went out together many times and he kept on telling her that he wanted a long life partner. He proposed to her unofficially, saying that his mother wanted him to get married soon and give them a grandchild. He never took her to see his parents but he was ready to go with her to see her own parents. Yvonne did not bother much about knowing his family or where he came from. She was not worried about his job because he had boasted that though he did not have a steady job, his uncles who were in Europe would help and besides, he did not look like a hungry person. They laughed over it and continued to date each other.

When her father insulted him during their visit, he decided to call off the friendship, but Yvonne encouraged him and they went and stayed in a one room apartment he rented in the Quarter. He used to raise her hopes that his uncle in America would sponsor him when he got married.

'Mama I was completely blind and I trusted him and gave deaf ears to my father's advice,' she wept loud and then continued.

'Then when I became pregnant, things changed. He stopped calling me as he used to when he was out of the house. He started coming back late and giving reasons that someone delayed him. During the seventh month of my pregnancy, he came home one evening and told me that he was going away for few days with some friends because he had a deal to settle. He never came back.'

'I wonder how you sorted out your bills when you gave birth?' asked her mother.

'Some of my friends especially Eileen helped to pay the hospital bill when the child was born. There was no way to contact Ben until now. I could hardly believe what had happened that Ben could abandon me like that. It was like waking in a dream.'

'Why did you not call me or come home?'

'Mum, I was afraid of dad. Eileen offered to come and plead on my behalf but I did not have courage to accept her offer, but mama, God sent Peter to come and rescue two dead bodies. I did not hear all the hard knocks at the door. I only struggled to get up when the fever was too much for the child and he started crying. I was too weak to care for myself. I had already given up and then found myself awake in the hospital. I had no clue how I arrived there. Peter said that I walked to the hospital but I doubted it. He must have carried the baby and me.' She knelt down crying aloud.

'Mama, papa e fit forgive me?'

'Clean your eyes. People learn the truth of life on the altar of hardship. You have made a mistake but what matters now is the lesson which you have learnt from your mistake. You have to forgive yourself first. You cannot change what happened. However, you can change your perception of what happened. You have acquired a new insight into the realm of life that can change your choice in life. I will talk with your father when he comes back and we shall see how you can move on with your life.'

Joe came back after one week. He saw Yvonne and said nothing. When he had finished his supper and went into the sitting room to listen to the news, Mary went to chat with him.

'I have something to talk to you about,' she began.

'What is it? I hope it is not about Yvonne because I am tired.'

'Yes I am aware that you are tired but I know that you may not be here tomorrow so we need to give her another chance.' 'No, not this night,' said Joe.

'Okay let's talk about something else. Tell me about all your mischief when you were a young boy. Your mother used to tell me how tough and rough you were.'

Joe smiled 'I will tell you the stories another day.'

'Girls used to run around you like flies and you were very proud and stubborn,' Mary continued stubbornly. 'I remember one who insisted that you must marry her before you saw me. Tell me, how did you unhook yourself from her? What is her name again?'

He now laughed and said, 'Those days when boys were strong!'

Musing over the past, he remembered Jessica and Cornelia who fought on their way to the stream because of him. He used to like Jessica very much but after she fought with Cornelia and tore her dress like a dog, he became afraid of her. He was really scared and ran away. He could not stand women fighting like lions. It was very scary. It was not common to see girls fighting with such anger and venom. She also beat her brothers. Many boys respected her but they dared not approach her for friendship. They used to call her ' Kumba breed.'

'How did you break off then?'

'Hm, it was not easy. I faked a story that my mother had got someone for me to marry against my will. Jessica did not find it funny but thank God someone else from another village came for her hand in marriage soon after. And I left home to start my training in the army camp. When I came back from holidays, I saw you on your way back from school. You were simple in a navy blue skirt and white shirt.'

He turned to her and said,

'You looked very innocent at that time and my heart beat a step faster and I knew that that girl walking there would be mine.' They laughed.

'I was sure that you would accept me because I was very aware of my fine features and pride. Then to my disappointment, you wanted to play a tough lady which was good any way.' They laughed.

'I thought your love was love at first sight. Thank God you did not run away when I refused your proposal. I would not have known how to trust men again,' Mary responded.

He could recall many girls he had dated and how they believed him very easily. He used to amuse himself whenever he teased a girl and she would follow him. They were gullible, easily convinced and taken over by sentiments and fabulous meaningless words and empty promises.

'It is senseless to believe that someone would see you for the first time and fall in love with you,' Joe said amusingly.

'But some people are like that,' Mary came in. 'but how would you know among the lizards the one that has stomach ache. That is why you should consider your daughter and give her a second chance.' Joe sighed

Mary continued,

'Please my love, forgive her, she has realized her mistake and has come home. It was actually Peter who saved her life. The boy abandoned her and went into thin air.'

'That serves her right,' retorted Joe. 'I could not understand how my own daughter could not listen to me and she thought life was a bed of roses. That is the reason she could not study. If I have spent the amount of money I gave her on Sledge and Peter, they would have gone far in their careers by now. The saying holds well here that you may be from the same parents but your destiny is different. You can send the cow to the river but you cannot force it to drink.'

Mary felt that it may be good to enrol her to learn handiwork like hairdressing or sewing since education was not for her, but they would discuss this with her to know what she was capable of doing.

'Who will take care of her child? She has to sit down and take care of the child or send him to the orphanage.' suggested Joe.

Mary recalled vividly the day she visited the orphanage.

The stone building sat in a corner of the compound, not far from the building where the care givers lived. She walked through the deserted building, imagining the anguished children who would live there and grow up without their mothers and without an identity. The compound was a bit neglected. Some of the children were crying seeking attention to be carried, but the nurses were limited and overworked. She remembered how she stood at the entrance door and listened to the echo across the empty hall as many children were yelling. The smell inside was a horrid combination of urine, faeces, and neglect. Children flooded out of the rooms. This section contained about forty boys whose ages varied from toddlers to teenagers. In the other section were the girls. They probed Mary with chapped hands, clamouring for attention. Their clothes were apparently whatever could be found that suit their lanky bodies. Some of them were all eyes and bones. Some had open sores on their arms, legs and faces. They hardly had enough to feed them. A Sister in charge of the centre saw the look on her face and gave little explanation.

'This is actually one of the better places. We've worked hard to make it liveable but as you can see, we have a long way to go.'

'There is not enough space as about ten children are brought in every day, with no money, except for what the relief organizations and few church groups throw our way. The government does little, the churches next to nothing.'

Mary sighed and said to her husband.

'Often the women are blamed for abandoning those children without a thought to the father who abandoned both the mother and the child without a thought to the circumstances that led to that decision of abandonment. No, she has had enough traumas already. I will take care of the child so that Yvonne can start her life anew. I would not like to send my first grandson to the orphanage while I am still alive.'

The discussion ended on that note. The next morning Yvonne met her father and pleaded on her knees for forgiveness. A father's love never dies. Despite his pain and disappointment, Joe still loved his first daughter dearly. It was true she was not as sharp and intelligent as others but it goes to confirm the belief that each person created has his or her own unique plan which nothing can change till it is fulfilled. Joe was ready to pay for Yvonne's training to learn either hairdressing or sewing. In fact, he was ready to train her to become a professional.

Yvonne decided to learn sewing and become a seamstress. Their mother met Cecilia, one of the seamstresses she knew in town and she was enrolled.

Yvonne learned her lesson the hard way. She never wished to set eyes on Ben again.

The mother took care of her grandson with all devotion. She did not yield to the criticism and inquisitiveness of her neighbours and colleagues in the school.

'Mary I did not see you with child but you have a baby, did you adopt one?'

Asked one of the teachers

'Yes, I have been given another child to show love.' Mary would answer. And they would expect her to say more, but she never did.

The gossip went on for few months and died away. There were people in life who found their joy only when they were talking about other people's lives but they dared not talk about themselves or let others see through them. They were the busybodies who found joy in others' sad events. One could never rely on them. Their mouths were like baskets that could not hold water. She knew them among the teachers. Most often they had no peace in themselves or in their homes but they tried to fix the problems of others thereby setting discord and division.

The next day Sledge came home with her own story.

5

Sledge's Experiences

S ledge came home from Mesong-Mesala during the weekend and narrated her dramatic experience in the job she had had for one month. She had got a job after one year of endless struggle- the job had caused her lot of pains and left her penniless. All along, she felt that there was something odd about the way the job was offered to her. She burst out surprisingly to her mother and herself,

'The morning I met Mr Tom in the corridor was the best morning and the worst of mornings.'

That statement attracted their mother's inquisitiveness she looked at her like a confused person and asked which it was? 'Was it the best or the worst because it would not be possible to have been both?'

Ordinarily Sledge would have laughed at herself and agreed with her mother, but the truth was that the morning when she met her boss Mr Tom in his office in Mesong-Mesala *was* the best and the worst of her life.

She was beside herself when Mr Tom offered her a job in the finance department without a struggle or expense. It was a job many people with good degree results had struggled to get for many years. She thought she was the luckiest girl in the world. She immediately withdrew all the other applications she had sent out.

There were many people standing in the corridor that day - all of them young people looking for a job. Many were graduates and she had not expected to get the job but with her knowledge of computers and linguistics she decided to take a chance all the same. The department needed a secretary who had knowledge of computer and filing, and as an added qualification, the person must be able to speak French and English. Sledge stood with her friend Joy chatting over many things that had happened in the college.

All of a sudden the door opened and Sledge was beckoned into an office. She was afraid and unprepared to go for the interview. Many people had come earlier and had taken their numbers. They were among the last group. She looked back but no one moved.

'La dame en jupe noir et rose, oui, venez ici,' blathered the man in French.

She looked at her friend Joy who encouraged her to go on.

Sledge entered the room, muttered greetings to the man who called her.

She was faced with another man sitting on a big office chair with his hands resting on the table in a carefree manner. She greeted him in French, 'Bonjour monsieur'

She remembered that she had seen him pass in the corridor several times that morning. He raised his head and looked straight at her without answering her greeting. She greeted him again shyly. He nodded and fixed his eyes on her. A colleague of his entered from the adjoining room and joined in devouring her as if she was a piece of a sculpture carved for an exhibition. She kept her eyes low on the floor. She was beginning to melt beneath the knees when Mr Tom spoke up.

'Young lady, may I know your name.'

'My name is Sledge.'

He smiled and seemed to chew the name as he rolled his tongue in his mouth and then said 'Sledge is a nice name and

52

it fits your features.' He was quiet for what seemed like ages before he went on in a self-assured tone.

'Vous parlez bien le français et l'anglais?'

'Oui Monsieur, Je parle bien le français et l'anglais.'

He smiled and spoke in English again.

'Now there are many of you standing out there at the corridor waiting to be interviewed. I would not have the time to go through all the processes of calling one person after the other.' He paused and continued, 'I think you can make a good secretary if you meet our requirements- namely knowledge of computer, linguistics, and office filing. You must also be smart and ready to work.' He rolled his tongue again.

Sledge answered respectfully that she was proficient in English and French and that she had knowledge of computers but she had not done office filing. Her heart missed a beat when she declared that she had no knowledge of office filing for she remembered that Joy told her to answer 'yes' to any job in the office. However, her fear was averted by Mr Tom's responses after sometime,

'Oh that is pretty good. You can easily learn filing if you work for a few days in the office,' and the interview was over for the day. He asked her to, 'come the next day to collect your appointment letter and bring your curriculum vitae.'

She was not sure what he said next, for she was overwhelmed and stupefied.

She muttered, 'merci Monsieur,' and she came out still confused.

Joy ran to her to find out why she stayed so long. The people in the corridor were already murmuring and complaining that her interview had lasted too long. The interviews seemed to be over. She was dumbfounded. She walked down the corridor and Joy was nosey to know what had happened. She was just as confused as she was when she went in. She had mixed feelings of joy, fear and uncertainty. She told Joy what had happened and that the interviews were over. It was so strange that she was the only person who was admitted for an interview and the only one chosen. Joy was happy for her friend and could not comprehend why her friend was confused. Joy was a carefree girl who would not give a damn as to how or where she got a job. She would do anything to get money. She was the opposite of Sledge who was determined to keep her dignity at all cost.

The next day Sledge came and met Mr Tom in the same office. People were still standing around in the corridor hoping that the interviews would be resumed. She handed over her curriculum vitae. As he was going through her documents, she had time to observe him.

Mr Tom was a tall man, nearly three inches over six feet, with a rangy, disciplined build more accustomed in the last years to old tailored suits than the classical modern suit he wore that day. His hair was black. His face was lean, the long bones of his cheeks well defined. His eyes were alert and presented a dramatic picture. His stomach seemed big but it was shaped by his suit which gave it a funny flat shape. He seemed to use his looks to intimidate people when it suited him, just as he seemed to use charm to reach his goal. These observations made Sledge shiver where she was standing. Sledge felt he held in his hands the power to make people extremely unhappy.

'That is what I wanted,' Mr Tom said aloud as he looked up from the paper and smiled at her, 'you will be my personal secretary,' he told her.

On the first day of September, Sledge began work as personal secretary to Mr Tom. The first few days, he instructed one of the experienced secretaries to coach her on how to arrange files. When she walked into Mr Tom's office, she was full of admiration. The office was the epitome of superior quality. It had an imposing beauty and softness intermingled with gold and milky colours. The long glass windows were decked in light gold curtains that shaded the attractive garden and when they were opened, the room seemed to be part of the blue sky. One could hear the birds chirp as they move from tree to tree and saw the colourful butterflies that hop round the different coloured flowers. The flowers, which were designed artistically, gave the place an air of tranquillity.

Sledge's office was nice and small and lacked the luscious chairs and the refrigerator of her boss but she was comfortable and liked it.

'But mum you know I worked with Mr Tom for one month without getting paid,' she said tearfully.

'What happened then?' Yvonne was nosy to hear how the story ended.

One fateful day, Mr Tom called her into his office after one week and told her emphatically that he employed her because he wanted her to be his mistress. He fell for her when he saw her in the corridor waiting to be interviewed. Sledge politely asked him if he meant marriage. He laughed and told her that marriage was relative.

'Our relationship may end in marriage, one never knows the turn of tide,' he had said.

Sledge struggled to avoid his passes. She had turned down several invitations to dine outside with him. During break, Mr Tom came to her office and stood at the door. Sledge greeted him and continued her work.

'Miss Sledge would you like to grace me with your company today? We can have lunch together.'

Sledge was scared and could not look up. She stopped her work and searched for an excuse to give but none came to her. She suddenly muttered,

'Please Sir; I did not plan to go for break today. I really have a lot to type before the end of the day.'

'I see you are a very busy girl but you need time out for break, we will not be long, let's go.'

Sledge could not stop him from persuading her. She reluctantly got out of her seat. As she was about to pick her bag, the phone rang and she answered it. It was from the Governor's house and they needed Mr Tom urgently for some meeting. Mr Tom was not happy and complained that he was getting tired of those impromptu managers' meetings.

'Sledge, I am called out now, I will see what happens,' he came and held Sledge and gave her a peck. Sledge cringed at the touch of his hands.

'Oh they don spoil e man e plan.' Yvonne giggled. Sledge looked at her sister and continued the story.

The worst dramatic scene happened one afternoon; it was the last Friday of the month. All the workers had received their salaries in the morning. Sledge was supposed to be paid on that day like every other worker in the department. When it was ten minutes to the closing time, Mr Tom gave her letters to type. He told her that she must finish the letters before she went home for the day since it was weekend. All the workers left when it was time and Sledge had to stay to finish typing the letters.

Mr Tom came back at about quarter to 6 p.m. Sledge was on the last paragraph of the last letter. Mr Tom came and stood at her back. He was very imposing. He held her and ordered her to stop typing. She became nervous.

'I have been looking forward to the day you would be alone with me like this; now stop typing, pack the papers and let us go to my house. You will receive your salary there.'

She breathed deeply and looked up. He ogled at her smiling. She felt threatened.

'Please Sir,' Sledge murmured.

'Yes dear,' he answered.

'You know I respect you and I have a high regard for you because you have been kind to offer me the job. I wish you would allow this friendship to grow naturally to last long.'

'Thank you for your kind words. But you see I have prepared a nice meal for you in my house. You are a hard working girl and I want to say a real thank you today. I cannot accept such an officious advice from the one I wish to honour. You know I am very expensive,' he boasted, 'and not easily found by those who desire me but as nature would have made it, it is my desire to get acquainted with you.'

Sledge had made up her mind that she would not accept the invitation to his house. It was something of an oddity. She quickly searched for an excuse to give.

'I cannot go to your house sir, you are my boss. I have an appointment with someone,' Sledge said obstinately. Mr Tom ignored what he saw as a silly and offensive excuse and went on.

'Well if I am your boss, you have to do as I say. What is wrong in going to your boss's house?' he asked. His voice was imposing but Sledge refused to yield to it.

Then it occurred to her that they were alone. She got up quickly, packed the typed letters and handed them to him but he refused to take it insisting that he would only take them in his house.

Sledge left everything on the table and walked out of the office into the corridor. Her mind was made up. Mr Tom came out and told her to walk to the car. When she walked pass his car, he became furious and shouted.

'Sledge, if you do not enter that car, consider your job terminated without salary. You know this is the end of the month'. She could not obey that singular order.

At ten o'clock on Monday morning, Mr Tom came into the office, called her out to the corridor and handed her an envelope. She thought it was her salary but it was a letter of dismissal. All the other workers were surprised, but nobody could question the manager's decision.

That was how she lost her job. Sledge broke down at that stage and let off steam.

After she had cried for few moments, she continued the story of what happened next.

She went to Joy and told her what happened.

Joy was surprised at her behaviour and burst out,

'Sledge, don't tell me that you have given up that job just like that! Do you not remember how you struggled to look for jobs before you got that one? I do not have a job.

Je cours jusqu'u a l'arrivee, mais vous...

'You must be out of your mind to give up yours. If I were you I would have followed him to the house. The highest thing he would do is to have you and that's all and you get your salary. He would have been giving you more than your salary.'

Sledge replied, 'Joy what you said might be true but do you know what it means to be a mistress to a man who is your boss.'

'Oh! But what! Who does not know?' retorted Joy, 'I mean you are a fool. This is why I hate that church you go to.'

'This has nothing to do with church Joy' Sledge blurted out. 'It has more to do with conscience and consequence. I cannot be his mistress. Many things will go wrong if I accept that and eventually I will still be sacked.'

Joy became forceful, 'Nothing would go wrong, go back and ask him to forgive you. You cannot give up that prestigious job just like that; after all, the man is still single.'

Sledge would not yield to that voice. She told Joy that she preferred to be the wolf than the house dog.

'What do you mean by that?' queried Joy.

Sledge told her the story of the wolf and the house Dog:

One night a wolf met a dog. The dog was taking a walk but the wolf was looking round the dustbins in the hoping to find something to eat because he was very hungry.

'I wish I looked as well as you do!' said the wolf, 'What cruel weather! It's as much as I can do to stay alive.'

'Well,' answered the dog, 'why don't you take a job like mine? It is easy, and I am very comfortable.'

'Really?' asked the wolf.' 'What do you do?'

'Why, I just have to guard the master's house and keep burglars away. That's all.'

'I would be happy to do that,' the wolf said, 'I don't remember when I last had a good meal.'

'Come along with me then,' suggested his friend. 'I'll take you to my master and we'll see what he has to say.'

As they were trotting along together the wolf noticed a strange mark on the dog's neck.

'What's that? he inquired, 'have you had an accident?'

'Oh no, it's nothing,' replied the dog touching his paws on the spot.

'Do tell me—I want to know,' the wolf insisted, 'why do you have a mark on your neck?'

'It is because I wear a collar,' explained the dog casually. 'You see, I am chained up in the day time and let loose at night,'

'Chained up?' shouted the wolf in horror

'You will soon get used to it,' continued the dog, 'And think of all the petting you will get, not to mention the delicious food!' The wolf looked dismayed and began to hurry off as fast as he could run.

'Wait,' cried the dog. 'Where are you going?'

'I could not bear a chain!' the wolf called over his shoulder. 'Even if I am cold and hungry, I am free. I can do what I like. Goodnight!' and he disappeared into the forest.

Sledge finished the story and said, 'Joy, honestly, my freedom is better than a comfortable prison.' Joy told her to look elsewhere to stay because the room would no longer accommodate them both.

The next day she went out again in search of another job.

As she was walking on the streets of Mesong-Mesala, a car passed and stopped after a few meters. The driver wheeled back and stopped in front of her. It was Major General Abudullah, her father's colleague in the army.

'Are you Major Joe's daughter?' The Major asked her.

'Yes sir.'

'Hm how about your father and where is he'?

'My father has been posted to Furawa.'

'So what are you doing here since your father was transferred to Furawa?'

'I came to look for a job sir?' Sledge told him.

'And your father cannot help you. He is in a better position now.' He shook his head and told her to greet her father and drove off.

It was then that Sledge decided to go home and narrate her disappointments to her family.

Meanwhile Peter had been struggling to control his temper. He blurted out.

'I hate it when people take advantage of innocent people. That man is a devil in disguise. You have made a noble difference by not yielding to his demands.' Mum that is what it means to make a difference. I am proud of my sister. I know God will show the way. Where there is a will, there will be the way. When one door closes, God opens the window.'

Her mother praised her for her decision to quit the secretary job.

'That job is not meant for you, do not worry, you do not belong to that school of behaviour.'

Yvonne however had a different opinion. She said she would not have quit the job because the man seemed to be interested in her. She argued,

'Any man who invited a lady to his home must be serious now. If Ben had even allowed me to visit his parents, things would have been different.'

'No Yvonne, Mr Tom offered me the job for his own gratification; out of his impure desire to conquer, it was not true love. I am glad that I did not give him that power to abuse me.'

Yvonne retorted, 'Well, I did not really understand your point there. This is your boss and he asks you to dine with him because you have been working hard, I did not see anything wrong. It was better to go and see what would happen. If he makes unnecessary requests, you can refuse.'

'Hm, it is easier said than done, jamais' Sledge maintained her stand.

'You know him better,' said Yvonne. 'Maybe I trust people too quickly and they tread on my ignorance.' She sighed as her experiences flooded in her mind.

'I think that man is lucky that I was not there. You deserved to be paid for the month you worked for him. The justice in this country is nothing to write home about. I would have suggested that we sue him.' chipped in Peter.

'I thought of that but then I considered that it may take more money to get a lawyer and file your charge and more over I have no money and our dad is not the kind of person that would fight for me.'

'I will be a lawyer one day and I will have a say in the law and order' Peter promised.

'Amen,' Sledge and Yvonne applauded.

Sledge told their father about her encounter with Major General Abudullah and about his surprise at finding her looking for a job when her father could help her find one.

Her father told her that the man was an idiot.

'He is among those men in the army who squanders Government money without a qualm or the wink of an eye and employs any idiot to any post so far as they agree to give them half of their salary or collect money on the road for them. Such men should be avoided, in fact, eliminated. Their likes are the social chameleons,' he went on. 'You could only get a job by merit and not by favour. Jobs gotten through such favours always end very badly either one party could be indebted forever to the other or not. It often comes with a pound of flesh.' Joe added.

'What is the meaning of 'social chameleons?' asked his wife.

'Social chameleons are those who do not mind in the least saying one thing and doing another if that will win them social approval. They simply live with the discrepancy between their public face and their private reality. To get along and be liked, they are willing to make people they dislike think they are friendly with them.' He finished and added, 'Tommy and I were always at cross- roads when we met each other in the army camp.'

He suggested to her to go and learn hair dressing. Sledge begged him to send her back to school, but he complained that he had no money. Even the money to learn hairdressing was not assured. Peter felt sad for his sister and said,

'Dad I do not really like the way you treat Sledge and me. What have we done to you? Look at what has happened to Sledge and still you cannot support her. Everybody says you can help and yet you don't.'

'If you depend on me you waste your time because I have no money. Feeding you all is a big job already. If I had only two children instead of all these hungry mouths depending on me things would have worked better. I would train them to the University level.'

'Ha, is it children's problem. Did they ask you to give birth to them? They deserve to be cared for,' came in Mary.

'I am not ready for this, you can train them if you like,' Joe walked out of the room.

Sledge left her father more disappointed than when she arrived and went to stay with Peter.

6

Peter

Meanwhile Peter gained admission to the University of Eklewindi after two years of working and writing advanced level as an external candidate. He had four papers in the advanced level and he gained admission to the law department in the University of Eklewindi. He worked hard that month and made some money that would pay part of his fees.

Unfortunately, thieves went to his room when he was at work and stole all his things and the little money he had earned. Peter came home and found his back window wide open. He lived in a small bungalow in one of the villages in Mpongo. It was not a modern building as most of the buildings in that part of the village were built with mud blocks and bamboo sticks. His window which was made of a plank had been pulled out by the thieves as they made their way into his room. They turned everything upside down and took his money from where he had hidden it under his bed. When Sledge came back from the market she met her brother crying.

'What is the matter?' Why are you crying? Did somebody die?'

'No, thieves came to the house.'

'Thieves, how did they enter?'

'Through the window and they took all my money. I have been saving this for the past three years. Now I cannot begin my studies next week as I planned.'

'Oh that is terrible; I know it must be those crazy and lazy boys roaming about this area doing nothing. What are we going to do now?'

'No this was an organized robbery because those idiots had enough time to scatter all my things. They know when I go out and when I come into the house.'

'I suspect that plumber who comes at odd times to do repairs for the landlord. He looks like a devious man.'

'I don't know but I think it is time to leave this place. There are many idle boys loitering around and one never knows what they are up to.'

'I think it is a good idea. Let's go and stay near the University.'

'Yes, I think I will leave this place and move to Eklewindi. I am foolish too to have kept my money here. I should have saved my money in the bank. Now I have to defer my admission and that is the most painful part of it.' he sighed.

'Can we call the police or tell our parents,' asked Sledge.

'No, there is no need. I would have loved to tell our mother but she may not be able to help financially. I don't know what dad does with his money anyway.'

'He is not interested in how we succeed in life but we will succeed. The power within is stronger than his neglect.'

'Do you believe that the power within will conquer neglect?'

'The power within me is filled with love and justice. The power to make choices and work towards its realization is my driving force. As you said we will leave here and find a better job and place in Eklewindi.'

Peter felt sad because it meant he would not take his place in the law school as he had planned. He deferred his admission for another year while he continued to work.

When he went out the next day, he met Ngong as he was returning from his work. He was dressed in black trousers tucked in neatly with a nice white shirt and a beautiful black tie. He wore glittering shoes that gave away their long term use because one could notice that black colour on top covered the original colour. Though they looked attractive they had a superficial quality. He looked like a fake young banker without an office.

Peter was very happy to see his mate after three years of leaving school. Ngong feigned his movement and walked with ease and contentment towards Peter, a sign of one who was happy with his situation. Ngong inquired about his life.

'Peter, what type of job have you been doing all these years?'

'Well, I have engaged in a lot of jobs: I have been motor boy for six months, that did not work, I joined the car washers but it was not steady and at times I got work with the cocoa company or work on people's farms but it was not always available as many people are into the same job. As you know it yields only a little pay. It has been a struggle from hand to mouth,' he sighed.

Ngong laughed and asked him 'Peter, how would you make a difference in your life with the kind of jobs you do. I thought your father would have helped you. He is a big man in the army.'

'My father is not the custodian of my future. My future is in my hands and I will make it to education.'

'Education, so you have not given up the idea of education?'

Ngong boastfully told him about his political party,

'We have been moving from one end of the country to another campaigning on political affairs. The forth coming election will surely favour our party; the new Prime Minister will surely come from my town.'

'So what is the point of your hope and where do you belong in this running around? However, it is not the political party that will build your future for you because life is not just about politics, but also fulfilling your aspirations in life.'

Ngong smiled.

'My aspiration is to be the next President of this great nation. I will work and exercise all my strength to arrive at my dream. The power within is controlled by money. Money is the master. Yes, the president of our group has said that I will be made the Public Relations Officer during the next coming election; I have already planned how I will align all the other political groups so that we have one large group called A. P. E. P. (All Peoples Empowerment Party). Hopefully, if that works out, I will be given a four wheel drive car for my work.' He laughed ironically.

'Oh that sounds farfetched.' Peter wondered how an illiterate mind like Ngong could be the Public Relations Officer for such an important opposition party. From his experience, Ngong did not possess the relational qualities he talked about. He was an empty gong that made the loudest noise. And he said to him,

'Hm Ngong, if I were you, I will begin now to think about the future. You are holding on to nothing really, you are neither intelligent nor clever though you have a bit of chameleon- like characteristics but that alone cannot …?

Ngong did not allow him to finish and burst out,

'Peter, I know that we never agree on anything. I don't even know why I stopped to speak with you. You always think that you know everything and you can fix everyone. Common sense should have told you that you cannot fix me. Get away foolish boy.'

'Ngong, one thing with you is that you do not listen to reason and the saying that the deaf fly follows the corpse to the grave, holds good for you here and I…'

Ngong went to fight him.

'Oh you are calling me a dead corpse? Has it come to that? I will teach you a lesson today.'

Before Peter could move, blows landed on his back. Peter resisted the urge to fight back. He turned and Ngong held him by the collar of his shirt. Other boys moving round came and dragged Ngong's hands off his shirt.'

'Next time you insult me, I will tell you that I am a politician. Idiot'

Peter looked at him and said,

'Two people cannot be mad at the same time,' and walked away.

'You are the mad one,' Ngong shouted as other boys tried to drag him away.

Peter moved to Eklewindi with Sledge and he got a job in one of the computer shops. He learnt how to help customers to browse and work on Microsoft Word and Power Point. Being a clever boy, he learnt how to repair some minor faults in computers. He found favour with the manager and worked there for one year until he earned enough money to pay his first year fees at the University. The fees were not expensive but he had to pay for accommodation, food, clothing and other things.

He stayed in the school accommodation which was not too expensive.

The University was one of the best in the country with its v-shaped design. The compound was decked with dwarf trees from the gate to the academic blocks, the hostels and then the car parks. The lecture rooms were provided with modern furniture and were well equipped to suit their purpose. People used to look at the campus and comment,

'Government don bury all we money for here o.'

It was the first time the school had run the medical school. The only standard medical school in the country was in Mesang-Mesala. Eklewindi was opened to decongest the medical school in Mesang-Mesala and moreover it was situated in the English speaking area, so many people who longed to study medicine saw it as a big opportunity to fulfil their heart's desire.

The interior was luxurious and was elegantly furnished with all the chemical, scientific medical equipment and material to suit a modern science laboratory. The Theatre was situated at the left side of the building. The architectural design was an archetype which not only attracted young people to study medicine but also attracted tourists from other countries. Its creation caused a bit of unrest in the country.

There was a riot in the University. Problems began after the entrance examination to the medical school came out. Five hundred people entered for the examination and three hundred and fifteen passed but the school could accommodate only one hundred and sixty candidates.

The university decided to interview the first two hundred and chose one hundred and sixty candidates from amongst them. On the morning of the interview, people discovered that the list had changed overnight. New names were added to the list and some names of those who actually passed were missing from the list. There was uproar in the university and the interviews could not be continued. It was rumoured that a list came from nowhere to the medical department urging the Vice Chancellor to admit the list of candidates from Mfoum Division without further interview. There were 60 names.

Students felt that it was absurd for such a thing to happen and could not tolerate such dubious business.

The president of the student's union gathered the students together and they decided to boycott lectures until the university brought out the original list that contained the names of those who had passed and were listed for interview. Everyone seemed to have seen the original list before it went missing. The students blocked the entrance to the university, preventing people from either coming in or going out. A riot was imminent.

The Vice Chancellor claimed that he was not aware of the new list.

Peter decided to move down to the university gate to see what was amiss. A student he met running back from the gate told him to turn back.

'Do you not know that the University gate had been blocked?' said the student.

'I know but why can't people go out? I mean we are not doing anything here.'

'You may go but it is not safe. The students have locked up the gate and the police are arguing with them there.'

Peter continued moving down to see for himself. He smelt the tear gas and stopped. Then he saw people running away from the direction of the gate. Peter wanted to know what was going on. He knew that the students had boycotted lectures and most of them were standing around the campus gate. He wanted to join them. Then more people ran up and he heard the gun shots and dreadful shouts. Students were screaming. A student had been shot and blood was pouring out of his mouth like water running from a tap.

Others flew away but Peter ran to the scene and picked the wounded student up and shouted

'Students please help!' The police from Mesong-Mesala and Nanga- Eboko had joined those from Eklewindi, shooting into the air. One of the police came and slapped him while he was holding the wounded student and shouted at him.

'You have to save yourself first. Get away. Let him die.'

'No why are you shooting us? I cannot let him die.' He started shouting 'students help help!'

The other policeman kicked him in the back.

Some of the boys who saw what was happening were prodded into action and ran in a rush, 'Kill us. We are ready to die,' shouted the students as they ran to help Peter. The two police men moved quickly away when they saw the students coming. They carried the boy to the taxi and took him to the hospital. Peter sustained a slight pain on his back where the policemen had hit him. He received medical attention as well.

The news went round like wild fire that the police had killed two students. This provoked the students and they started throwing stones at the police.

The armed forces were sent from the capital city to disperse the students. They used tear gas and scattered the students. Some soldiers opened fire on the students as well. The students fought back and some were wounded and a few lost their lives. The students refused to be dispersed. The university had to close and students were asked to leave the campus.

Some of the lecturers supported the students. The Chancellor of the University closed the university for more than one month to sort out the problem.

Other universities in the country had peaceful demonstrations for two days, some for a week in solidarity with their sister University. It was a big concern for the whole country because such a thing had never happened before. There were a lot of underground plans that missed the eyes. And the students wanted to seize the opportunity to address the inequality between the French and the English speakers of Cameroon.

When the students came back, they discovered that the Vice Chancellor had been removed and another lecturer was enthroned in his place. That posed confusion for the students. It was difficult to know how the problem was settled.

There was rumour that the original list was used while others felt that the interview was not free and fair as the result was made known privately to those who had passed and the public was left in the dark.

Peter felt sad that at times public opinion was treated like trash. It made it difficult to stand up for the truth. That was where colonial activities showed their wicked faces. The colonial masters introduced divide and rule games to disintegrate the people who had one mind and one heart. Since then, there had been that underlying hatred between tribes in Cameroon. They often felt that people from Nanga-Eboko and Mesong-Mesala had advantages and privileges that they could not have.

At the end of his second year in the University, Peter was chosen by consensus as the new students' union president. Peter knew that he had been outspoken in lectures, arguing intelligibly on issues concerning law and order in the country, and in the world at large, but it never crossed his mind that the students loved him enough to elect him as their president. He contested with two other guys in other departments but got 80% votes. People recognized among other things, how he stood out for the student who was shot during the riot.

During his regime as the president of the students' union, he was very active. He introduced new things like helping students to obtain student loans in the university. He was able to convince the authorities and created part-time job opportunities for students on the campus. He attended most of the meetings inside and outside the university and updated the students on current affairs.

Peter missed some of his lectures and depended on his friends' notes to catch up with the work. He worked round the clock to keep up with the academic demands and his union work.

He got into problems with one of the lecturers in the department who was unhappy with him missing some of the lectures. Though he passed his exams, one lecturer in particular felt that he needed to be punished for missing those lectures.

Peter had just come back from one of the inter-university meetings really worn out. He sat on his bed and kicked off his shoes and threw his shirt on top of the chair. He was too tired even to eat and decided to have a little nap but as he put his head down on the pillow he heard a knock on his door. He reluctantly got up again and was taken aback when he opened the door and saw one of his lecturers, Miss Ode. Before Peter could mutter a greeting, she said:

'Meet me in my office tomorrow because you have to prove to me how you will graduate at the end of the year,' and she walked away quickly.

Tiredness disappeared from Peter and was replaced with anxiety. Normally, lecturers did not come to the hostels of students; they would send someone to give a message or call the student if there were a problem. It was surprising that Miss Ode had traced his room by herself.

The next day Peter went to her office and she was not there. He looked for her for one week but could not find her. One day he bumped into her on the landing near the library and wanted to find out the best time to meet her but she passed him by quickly.

Peter decided to follow her after a lecture. Miss Ode saw him following and moved faster and purposefully as if she was rushing to meet the last bus. He insistently followed her till they arrived at the door of her office and then she turned to him sharply and said,

Mr President, you are late. I sent for you more than a week now, but you are too big to come. Do not try to sit for my papers because you will fail all the same. You have missed my lectures for three sessions and I cannot pass you no matter what you write. One of the rules of the university is that you have to attend all your lectures.'

'Yes Miss, please let me explain…' came in Peter but he was interrupted. She waved him away and continued.

'You have to prepare yourself to repeat the year,' she entered the office and closed the door.

Peter wondered what he was going to do. How could he repeat a year because of one paper? However, he was prepared to take the examination. He had studied that particular course well.

He went to the head of department and reported what had happened. The head of department, Mr Acha , was surprised that Miss Ode had not reported the case and wondered how she intended to stop Peter from taking the examination for her course. Such cases were normally discussed at the departmental meeting. He told him that he would bring it up at the meeting if Miss Ode did not bring it up herself. Meanwhile he told Peter to write a statement explaining why he had missed the lectures and to bring it to him.

The university authorities were aware that sometimes the president of the students' union had to attend important meetings away from campus for the wellbeing of the institution. The university was supposed to compensate him for missing lectures in the public interest.

'Leave the case to me,' he told Peter.

Peter's case was discussed at the departmental meeting but he did not wait for the outcome.

Peter believed that no matter how right he may be, he could not rub shoulders with his lecturer. He wrote a beautiful apology letter to Miss Ode and also explained his regrets for missing those lectures and promised to do his best in the future.

Miss Ode was pleased and she invited him to her office.

Peter arrived there at half past five in the evening.

'Well, you reported me to the departmental head,' she said.

'I am sorry Miss, I did not know how else to go about it. That is why I apologized to you.'

'Yes, I got your apology letter but that is not enough. I noticed that you are liked by the students. How many girlfriends do you have?'

'I have many good friends but I do not really have anyone I will claim as my girlfriend.'

'You mean to tell me that you have not fancied any of these girls copying notes for you?'

'No Miss, no one copies notes for me. I borrow their notes to copy myself.'

'I see. So what do you think of the general law?'

'I think it is good. I like it and I would like to specialize in criminology.'

Miss Ode smiled and said 'I need to see more of you. You can attend the examination but you must work hard for it.'

'Thank you Miss, I am very grateful.'

Peter faithfully attended her lectures. But one fateful morning, he got a note from Miss Ode inviting him to her office at the evening time. Peter wondered what the lady wanted from him again. It rained heavily during the day and he had planned to study in his room since he had no lectures that day. At about quarter to six in the evening his phone started ringing. He picked the phone but could not recognize the number. He answered all the same.

'Peter where are you.' The voice rang a bell. It was Miss Ode.

Peter was surprised that she had his number.

'Good evening Miss,' he responded.

'You are supposed to be in my office now, are you on the way?'

Peter hesitated.

'Are you coming or not?' it was an imposing tone.

'Okay Miss, I am on my way.'

As soon as Peter appeared, she stopped what she was writing, and questioned him.

'You have not been coming as often as I told you. What is the problem? Why do you avoid me? I do not see any girl moving around you and you do not want to be close to me.' Peter was silent.

'I often wonder what goes on in this mind of yours. Are you still annoyed that I brought you up at the departmental meeting?

'No I have ended the case and I thanked you for forgiving me.'

'What is the problem now?'

'Miss, I have a friend who is studying abroad and we communicate quite often.'

Hm, so you think that that friend is still waiting for you over there? We can still be friends, can't we?

'I really find it difficult to accept your proposal. I feel that we are on a different level. I am your student and…'

'Stop, I know, but I am interested in you. What is wrong with being my friend?

'I am sorry Miss.'

'Sorry for what? I would like you to think about it and give me a reply.

'Okay Miss.' Peter turned to leave. 'Eh come back,' retorted Miss Ode.

'Give me a hug before you go.' Peter was very shy.

Peter reflected over this incident and thought that he must be tactful with Miss Ode or else she may jeopardize his career. Before their final examination, he bought gifts and sent to her and thanked her for her care and concern. Miss Ode thought that it was a clear sign of acceptance and responded with gifts as well. Peter was confused.

That night Peter was woken up by a phone call from Irene, his girlfriend.

'Irene, from where are you calling?' he enquired.

'Ee I am still studying in Nki'Mbang now, have you forgotten me so soon?' she queried.

'No, it has been long since I heard from you. You have been enjoying life in white man's country and forgot poor people like us,' he teased laughing.

'No, things have been tough. It has not been easy here. You know, I work as well as study. My father said that I must struggle like other students.'

'So you have a part-time job like me, but the difference is that you are paid well when you work, unlike here, where you are hardly paid what you worked for and often they delay the payment for weeks.'

' That is injustice really, no, here you are paid promptly though some of my friends especially those doing support work claim that they are not often paid promptly, I don't know really. Have you heard of John's predicament?'

'John? Which John? We had three Johns' in our class.'

'I mean John Kumbo, the Senior Prefect and the best goal keeper in our class.'

'Oh! What happened to him? I heard that he went to Nki'Mbang to read Medicine.'

'Yes. He was to go to Germany but I did not know what happened and he landed here. Anyway they brought him home in a casket last week.'

Peter shouted, 'What!'

He was the victim of an attack that, even by the standards of a city battling against the blight of knife crime, is among the most horrific in living memory. His body was found late on Saturday morning, bound, gagged and with hundreds of stab wounds, and other injuries. He had been tortured and stabbed repeatedly with a blunt instrument. The police had still not been able to trace the culprit up until the time his remains were brought home.'

'John had finished his studies as a medical doctor. He was brilliant and he was one of the best medical students in the University. He was actually preparing to return home to practice his profession in his home town when the incident happened.' She sighed; 'one wonders why a talented and gifted guy like John would be killed.'

He was one of the brightest students in our class. He was actually one of the best senior students the school had recorded', Peter said in-between tears. They paused.

Irene told him that some parts of the country were difficult and dangerous places to live in. Youngsters moved around with knives and sharp instruments and they could corner unfortunate people and kill them even during the day.

'But one never heard about these things in the world news.'

'Who likes to wash his dirty linen in the market?' retorted Irene. All countries in the world have the same problems of violence, war, delinquency, bad government and other crimes. Do not be deluded by the World News continuous condemnation of the African Continent. There are many good things about us. But I must acknowledge the fact that there are areas where they have developed more than African countries especially in the areas of respect and provision of the basic human needs and social needs for their own people. They are still deficient in the upbringing of their children, and that can be one of the reasons why many young people leave home to join street gangsters.' She wondered how those children survived during winter out there in the street as it was very cold.

'It is sad to lose an intelligent guy just like that,' thought Peter.

However, Peter was happy to connect with his friend again and told her all that had happened to him and about Miss Ode's advances and his coming graduation. He also told her about his intending MA studies either in Sala or in Nki'Mbang but he was not sure where yet.

'Come and study here in Nki'Mbang. They have the best of education in Europe. I hope you have not dropped me and picked another girl. I know how they follow you like flies even the lecturers. What does the so called Miss Ode want from you?'

80

'No, you know I am a principled man. I have friends no doubt, but none has replaced you. More so, I cannot befriend my lecturer. You know it cannot work. Besides, I am afraid of losing you because I heard that girls cling to boys there because it is very lonely. I cannot comprehend how I would befriend my lecturer anyway but I am playing it cool because I would not like her to keep me in the university for another year.'

'Yeah, you need to be tactful there especially with a spinster. It is lonely here, but when you have somebody in mind, it keeps your spirit alight.' If you do not know what you came for then you can misbehave. I don't really have time for running around here, the young people drink and smoke too much. Some of the students get drunk almost every weekend.'

'They are true Cameroonians then.'

'No, not in that sense here when they have birthdays they rate the success of their friend's birthday by the number of bottles of beer she or he is able to take to get them drunk.'

'What type of culture is that?'

'It is not culture but, youngsters do funny things, you know. Not all of them oh. Some are respectful and cultured.'

'That reminds me of the meeting we went to last week in Yaoundé half of the students I went with filled their stomach with drinks and had a rough time. Some stayed for two days because they were drunk.'

'That sounds foolish. Peter I am looking forward to seeing you next year.'

'Yes, pray that all works out well for me.'

'Do you know what I miss most? The laughing African sun, the singing and chirping of birds and the swerving of the tall trees. I used to take these natural blessings for granted.'

'Are there no birds there to sing?'

There are but they do not sing like African birds and moreover, they migrate during the winter to a warmer climate. You see even the animals and things long for warmth.'

'Of course.'

'One does not value the gifts one has till one loses them.'

'Sometimes we remain blind to the riches around us.'

'Have a good night sleep and I love you.'

'I love you too, thanks for calling.'

Peter played his card well and made Miss Ode feel that he had developed an interest in her. He received more gifts from her. Peter sat for the examination. He passed and continued into his final year.

7

Social Insurance

Sledge lived with her brother for a year and half. She registered for a course in computer programming and acquired a higher diploma in it. She was very punctual and ready to give extra time when needed. Sledge was basically an honest person who saw things straight. She hated deception or deviousness; she needed to trust people because she often felt apprehensive about things. And she lacked the skills to follow lies and deception through it was not in her make-up. She had pains in her back whenever she tried to tell lies or hide something. Therefore she always took the narrow road and suffered the consequences that accompany honesty.

The Director of the programme appreciated her forward mindedness and honesty and employed her to work with them for a few months which was a rare privilege. She helped to retrieve some of the missing items in the office. She then registered to take her advanced level while working.

Sledge got a job at the social insurance department in Eklewindi. She worked in the office of the family allowance department. The offices were all together in a two story building. Each department had its own manager who was accountable to the director. The office of the director and managers were furnished with expensive furniture and decorations while the office of the clerks and others contained mainly tables, chairs and office furniture like drawers, files and office accessories.

The last weekday of the month was pay day for social services claimants. Often many people did not receive their

83

pay because it was alleged that their files were missing. Sledge discovered, to her amazement, loopholes in how pensioners' documents were handled by some workers and why some of the documents often got messed up or disappeared. Some documents were abandoned in drawers and nobody seemed to take notice except when there was a search or someone had given tips to the worker concerned. Some selected files were packed inside drawers which the workers visited only when they received tips from the owners of the documents.

Many files were never sent to the appropriate quarters for processing and signing.

She then understood why some people never got their pensions or their family allowance. While some received their benefits every month or quarter, others kept on sending one document after another. Sledge felt sad and shared her concerns with some of the workers. Some were not happy about the situation but felt that nothing could be done while some asked her not to dig into the case or else she would be digging her own grave. Sledge decided that whenever she finished her work in the office she would go to those drawers and retrieve the documents and send them to the appropriate quarters.

The whole system was flawed. There was a case of a man who had retired five years previously from the office of one of the Governors in the South West. He had worked as a clerk for 35 years. He prepared his papers and submitted them as soon as he retired. Every month he went there, he was told that the documents were incomplete. He kept on bringing one document after another till one day he met a new person in the office who told him that his file was missing. He was advised not to come for two months so that they could trace the file. It was after the two months had elapsed that he came and was complaining bitterly to another pensioner waiting on the corridor about his missing file and that he had spent a lot of money coming down from Kumbo for his pension. The entire file was nowhere to be found. No one seemed to be interested in his case. One of the workers boldly asked him one day:

'Papa have you got no son, ask your son to come and see the director or see us so that your file will move on and we can transfer it to Kumbo for you.'

Sledge overheard him complaining and decided to give assistance. She took the man and went with him to the pensioner's office. With the help of the new clerk, they struggled to trace the man's file from where the old worker had dumped it inside the drawer. It was discovered that nothing had been done in the file during the past five years since it had been submitted. Some of the documents were doubled. Sledge consoled the man and promised him that the file must move to Mesong-Mesala for processing and signing that week. It normally took two months or more for the files to return signed for payment. She told the man to give her his phone number so that she could call him when it was ready.

There were many cases of missing files that Sledge tried to retrieve. People began to ask for her whenever they came and she would go out of her way to trace their files and forward them to the director's desk.

There were some workers who despised Sledge for helping the pensioners. They found that people who used to come to them for such problems and whom they would ask them to pay some money illegally were no longer coming to them. Their cunning means of getting money almost crumbled. They warned Sledge to mind her own part of the office and not to meddle with other people's work. Sledge knew that to reason with such people was a waste of energy and reporting them to the director was even worse because he seemed to know what was going on and said nothing. Sledge claimed that some of the pensioners were from her area just to help them but it brought jealousy and hatred from others who were not happy that things were changing.

A year and six months after she started her job, she was transferred to Mfoum Social insurance office. Sledge felt bad because she missed the opportunity to help the needy. She was not going to give up helping. The people were unhappy when they heard about her transfer but they had no power to change it. They consoled themselves that since she was going near the headquarters she would be more useful to them if their files ever reached there.

In Mfoum, Sledge found that the situation was worse than in Eklewindi. Many workers did not even come to the office. There were many ghost workers. The insurance office was in a state of chaos. It was difficult to get any concrete information from some of the offices. However, there were a few people who did their job but they were like a drop in a bucket and were over worked. They tactfully did not discuss it or in any way let the cat out of the bag. Sledge discovered that a lot of money that was meant for the pensioners and family allowances went into the payment of the workers who did not exist. Then she understood the meaning of ghost workers. That was a huge problem in which she found herself. She started by trying to retrieve the papers of some who had been coming to her office crying about their files.

The director discovered that since Sledge had come to the office, he'd had more files to sign and approve. The number continued to escalate day in day out. He summoned her to his office and asked about the genuineness of those files and why there were more files now than before. She explained what she had found in her new office and how she had tried to retrieve the files that had been hidden away in drawers for years while the owners believed them to have been missing.

There was a particular woman who had five files. Each year she was asked to produce a new file because the old one was missing. The sad thing about the woman was that her name was recorded as one who had been receiving her pension for three years. No one could give an account of where the money went because the woman had never received any money.

Sledge noticed that the system of payment for pensions was deceitful because no one could discover whether they were workers or not. The money was paid directly into accounts and no one knew how authentic those accounts were.

It was a big eye opener for the director. He called a meeting of directors and managers and presented to them what had been discovered. He wanted them to create a ten man committee to look into the matter. There was confusion and one of the directors wanted at once to know who had discovered the case and had brought it to light. Some of them threatened the director who had raised the issue.

'If you do not tell us how you came about this discovery, we will not take part in this discussion. We need facts to be tabled clearly.'

Others argued that it would be good to set up a committee as he suggested investigating the authenticity of the allegation. But those who were involved in the crime and knew the seriousness of it refused to go further but tried to bring about confusion in order to drop the matter. One of them in particular, named Okon, threatened the director who called the meeting.

'Francis you should not forget the one who trimmed your tail during the rainy season. It is I, Okon who brought you to this company before you rose to the position of a director. You should be careful with what you see and say as far as the insurance office is concerned because you can still be thrown out at any moment. Do not be faster than your shadow.'

Mr Francis, did not expect such reactions from the directors whom he thought were very diligent in their work especially Okon his very close friend. Before he could open his mouth another manager spoke up in a rage.

'Francis or whatever you call yourself, there is a saying that the chick that does not listen to its mother's instructions hears them in the stomach of the eagle. He who gathers ant-infested maggots must be prepared for the visit of lizards. It is better to let the vicious sleeping dog lie.'

Many joined in blowing off steam and everywhere was turned upside down.

Some of the Directors ran away and some started beating Mr Francis. They beat him within an inch of his life and ran away before the police came onto the scene.

Some of the directors who were against Mr Francis mandated the managers to find out how the story came to light. They began their investigation from one department to another. They started with the taxation department, the pensions department, the social insurance department and finally the family allowance section, Sledge's department. There, they discovered that the files in the drawers were reduced compared with other departments. Spies were set up to trap the person and make things difficult. They discovered also that some of the ghost workers did not receive money in all of their accounts and that more pensioners received.

One day, the manager for the pension department called Sledge into his office and questioned her about the movement of files.

'How long do the files stay with you before you send them to the director?'

'I send the files to the director as soon as they are ready, Sir. There is no time limit mapped out.' she told him.

The manager praised her for her work and then told her that since she collected the money for the pensioners every month, she should bring it to his office for safe keeping before giving it to the owners. Some of the pensioners who did not have bank accounts preferred to collect their money in cash or send a relative to collect it on their behalf. Sledge could not understand the need for such a procedure of keeping the money in the manager's office and she questioned his suggestion. The manager said,

'Now I see, Sledge I think we have to make a deal. You know the washing of the left hand by the right hand is reciprocal. So next quarter I would like the payment for the pensioners to be delayed until the fourth quarter. This is what we normally do so that we do not give them the impression that money is always there and it also prevents the robbers from attacking this place.'

'In that case, Sir, I will inform the director,' replied Sledge.

The manager was enraged, 'so what I heard about you is true. You are playing with fire young lady. Get out of this office.'

Sledge knew that she was trapped and would lose her job if she did not comply. She made up her mind to ask for a transfer to another place. It was not easy to get such transfers unless they came from the authorities themselves.

A few months after this incident, Sledge received a letter of termination from her manager. The reason given for her dismissal was that the company needed to reduce the workers because there was no money to pay the many workers they had employed. However, only three workers were actually asked to leave.

Sledge had to lose the job not because they establishment could not pay their workers as they stated in the termination paper; the underlying reason was that Sledge did not comply with the manager plan to delay the payment of the salary of the workers till the next quarter. When the manager saw that she was not the kind of girl who would comply, he made a lot of complaints against her and eventually threw her out with two other unfortunate workers whose story she did not know. She took it with a pinch of salt knowing that she was not properly trained for public administration or accountancy. She could not stand up for her rights because she was not qualified. She promised herself that she would go and study accountancy and go back to that office. Once there, she would make a difference. She was a determined lady who never gave up in the face of battle.

Sledge's friend Festus who was working in the same company but in a different department was also used to getting into trouble. The manager blamed Festus for not engaging Sledge more often which gave her time to look at all the files and bring up old issues. Festus became very unruly and capricious to Sledge. He did not want to lose his job because of her.

Before then Festus loved Sledge and he was very respectful to her. He nursed the hope that their friendship might lead to marriage. When the problems erupted in the company, he started making unnecessary demands on Sledge. One day he invited her for an outing during work time. They used to go out together to have lunch or visit friends during their one-hour break or on the weekends. On that particular day, however, Festus decided they should leave their work and go to the beach in Kribi. Sledge could not understand the sudden revolt against work and why they should start their weekend on a Thursday.

Normally if they wanted to go away for a weekend, they would plan it together. They did not usually go for such long journeys because Festus did some private work on weekends. They argued for quite a long time and Festus walked away from her.

Sledge wondered what went wrong. Festus had never been as angry as he was that day. He accused her of things of which she was ignorant. He accused her of being authoritative, setting unnecessary boundaries in their relationship and always making him look like a fool and not like a man. All efforts to reason with him failed.

Sledge thought that she would talk with him later but there was no later. She called his house many times after work but could not find him. She tried to call him on the phone but he refused to answer her calls.

A few days after her dismissal she still had not seen Festus. She sent text messages but no reply came. She was devastated and decided to visit her parents. As she was packing in her room she discovered many letters written to her by Festus at the beginning of their relationship. She could not understand why Festus abandoned her and the reason for such unfounded demands on her at such a crucial time when she was in trouble. Some of the letters sounded so honest and real to her. She wondered why she had not noticed all that before that incident. It was a real contradiction in his behaviour. She read one aloud:

Dear Honey,

Can I walk the road alone? No, I need your helping hand: The hand I really love so much. I'll tell you a secret I have at my command. You are a special woman who came into my life. You entered it like the sunshine and warmed the cold within me. You helped me to unfold and to smile at life.

I'd like to share the rest of my life with you…'

Festus

There were lots of expressions about not being able to live without her in many of his letters and she wondered what had made him express those feelings and then change his mind at the slightest argument. She got annoyed for trusting him all along as a good friend but then she felt he was a nice person and was confused about his behaviour. The situation was beyond her.

She thought of writing an apology to Festus asking for forgiveness for whatever she had done wrong but there was nothing to apologise for. She decided to drop the issue having been convinced that others must have used him without his knowledge to make life more difficult for her. It was a very painful experience.

She met her friend Joy in the market when she went to buy things to travel home.

'Hi Sledge good to see you again. What brought you here?'

Sledge was not in the mood to share her problems with joy. She recalled how she drove her away after she was sacked by Mr Tom.

What have you been doing since we parted company?' asked Sledge.

'I have been living in a flat rented by one of the directors; accompanying him in his travels especially when he travels outside the country. He is very possessive of me and I love that. He is a married man but it is okay for me so long as he meets my needs.'

'I have known that it is your way of life, are you really happy?'

'Happy, what does a woman want in life? I have decided not to waste my life looking for a job that will not earn me more than I get from him or to wait for Mr Right.'

What about you? Joy queried.

'I am fine. I want to go back to school.'

'School, ha! I don't think I will ever go back to school. I just do not have the brain for it. I have moved on with my life.'

'Good luck.'

Sledge decided to seek admission in the University of Nanga-Eboko. She registered to do Accountancy. She had saved a little money which would pay her fees for the first year. She struggled hard and got work though it did not pay her much. It was difficult to get a job in the town. She was able to get menial jobs like cleaning and serving in the off-license bar and her knowledge of French was a big advantage to her.

She realized that life often presents a tangled twine that takes patience to untie. One must be careful not to break it during the process or else it will never be completed. The truth she came to realize was that life moved at a different pace for everyone and she vowed never to give up on life.

'Life remains at your beck and call so long as you do not give up when difficulties stare you in the face; it then opens a new chapter for the future. When one door closes, it paves the way for a better door to open. That is the irony of life.'

Sledge was positive that her life's ambition to study was becoming a reality. She was determined to go back to the insurance office after her studies and bring about the difference that lay within her. She did not hate the manager who expelled her but saw him as a fickle and narrow minded man who had darkened his mind with greed. She was consoled and encouraged by Peter when she told him how she lost her job.

'They that have the worldly powers need to be pitied most because the scale that barred their vision is a heavy one that cannot be seen with the ordinary eyes. They enjoy the fallowness of their empty lives while they wander through life like dreamers.'

8

Surprises for Yvonne

It was such a lovely day. It had rained the night before cooling off the hot sun that ravaged the day. The cool air made a welcome change after the intense heat of the previous day.

Yvonne went to work as usual. Her manager, Cecilia always insisted on punctuality. It was a big main market partitioned and arranged to accommodate various sellers all selling similar goods. The expanding spaces that separated the shades in a long row made it easier to zoom through the market without obstruction. There were lines for food, clothes, and electrical materials, building materials, household goods, handicrafts and a host of other things. The food and clothes sections of the market were particularly full. Although it sounded as though everyone was talking at once, it was still possible to hear one's neighbour or customers.

Cecilia's stall was remarkably full with many customers either collecting their sewn clothes or bringing new materials to be sewn. She was a disciplined lady and kept to the agreed time with every person who brought work for her. She had been a seamstress for the past twenty years. She was well known in the town as one of the best seamstresses specializing in women's traditional dress. Many young women had graduated from her workplace and it was a well-known place in the main market.

Cecilia could be heard in the midst of other voices exchanging greetings with one of her customers.

'Madam, I hope you are happy with your dress.'

'Yes you know how to sew shape into the material. I will be bringing all my dresses here for you. I like the way you respect and meet the promises you give your customers. Keep it up.'

'Thank you for your flattery.'

'No, you know if you do not sew well people will run away, but see, your stall is always full. I have to queue to see you and the trouble is that everybody wants to talk with you when they come to take their cloths. I will bring my daughter to learn from you.'

'Ok thank you.'

Cecilia had ten apprentices working in her care. She allowed apprentices one hour break every day except on the days they had more urgent work to do. They usually started at eight in the morning and closed at five in the evening.

Yvonne decided to rush home to see her child during the one hour break.

It was Tuesday afternoon. As she strolled down Central Avenue she let her thoughts about the work she left half-done ebb to the back of her mind so as to concentrate on her son. While she was looking forward to seeing her son, she was not sure whether her mother was at home or in the school. She had agreed with her that she would not go to the school to see her baby.

'People must not know who the mother of the child is though there is no smoke without fire. I do not want a situation that might prevent you from continuing your life as a single girl and may prevent other prospective suitors from coming for your hand in marriage,' her mother had explained to her.

Suddenly a car horn blasted through the tranquil afternoon, breaking her reverie, and realizing she had been dawdling, she quickened her step. It was then she became aware of someone walking behind her. The close proximity made her uncomfortable and she slowed down to let the person pass. But though the footsteps drew closer there was no attempt to overtake her. At first she tried to shrug it off- there were several people about, the traffic was still flowing, the parents and caretakers were all out to pick up their children from the schools. Nevertheless she stepped up her pace again and for a moment thought that whoever it was had turned off into the junction at the left that she had just passed. But as she reached the corner of the next junction and had to stop before crossing the road, a man came alongside her on the right. She kept her eyes fixed straight ahead, telling herself he was probably quite harmless, just taking a stroll home like her; but her hands were clenched tightly in her pockets.

To her horror, the man kept abreast of her and as they reached the other side of the road that was less busy she heard her name. Her eyes flew to his face and she opened her mouth to scream but nothing came out.

'No', he hissed. 'Please don't be frightened it is I.'

It was as if she had seen a ghost, and she blinked as he tried to give reasons and hold her at the same time.

Yvonne stared at him, her eyes achingly wide, and her heart thudding like a hammer. She tried to walk away but found she could not. It was as if she had suddenly been hypnotized.

'Yvonne, you have every right to be angry, I am not asking you to come back to me but I need the baby. My child, where is he?'

Yvonne could not believe what was happening, that Ben could have the guts to stand before her just like that. The anger welled over in her like a volcano ready to burst. The road had suddenly become empty. That was not her fear; she did not want Ben to follow her to the compound. If she had had a knife she would not have hesitated to use it on him. She gathered all her strength and shouted,

'You are not real, get out of my sight, as far as I know you are a ghost.' She pushed him out of her way and tried to run but Ben caught her and held her.

'Before you go, I want to inform you that I am taking the child away. I will come back soon, so be ready for me.' Then he pushed her a bit further from him and walked off.

When Yvonne arrived home there was nobody in the house. Her mother did not come home during the break because she took the child's food with her. She resisted the temptation to run to the school.

Yvonne returned to the office feeling very angry and then became alarmed and worried. She struggled to finish her work feeling sad. One of the apprentices inquired,

'Yvonne you do not look happy, did anything happen during your break?

Did you not have a good break or what?'

Yvonne sighed and said, 'I had an unpleasant encounter. The traffic was thick, but do not worry, I will be fine.'

' Ashia yaa.'

As soon as the time was up she went home and told her mother what had happened.

'How dare he approach you? The son of a bitch!'

'He want take my pikin.'

'Your pikin? He is a nefarious clever boy,' she paused and thought a bit.

'Ok, do you know what Yvonne, when he stops you again on your way, do not panic or shout at him, just ask him to come and see your parents and take the child so that I will teach him a lesson he will never forget. He will be made to pay for the damage done first.'

98

'Mum, he is a pauper, he has no job.'

'But he wants the baby; he must have the means to take care of him.'

'Woo to him if dad will be around on that day, he will come.'

'No, we are not going to inflict physical harm on him but he will learn the lesson of life. I am not surprised that he came to claim the child.'

'Mama, I am very surprised because he abandoned me before the child was born.'

'It is a terrible thing to do. He has to take care of the child because he is one of the parties that brought him into the world. The idea of taking him away is out of the question.'

'No I don't want him to see the child. Of course he had never seen him, so it is better not to. Mama I hate him,' she blasted out.

'I may not know how terrible you feel, but I know that many girls have been dropped like that. It is okay to feel hatred for him and I am glad you are able to express it as you are doing now. But as a biological father he must contribute to his up-keep and training, obviously he does not own the child.'

'Mama you do not understand how I feel. Ben wants my child and not me. He never loved me and my love for him is gone. I hate him now.'

'Yes, but if you do not allow him to contribute to his upbringing he will have it easy all the way.'

Mary spoke calmly, holding Yvonne's hand,

'My daughter, once a child is out of the womb, he ceases to be the child of the parents but everybody's. But it is still the duty of the parents to bring up the child. Where do you think your father and I will get money to bring him up when your father finds it difficult to pay your brother and sister's school fees?'

'Mama you cannot understand how it feels to be abandoned by someone you believe loves you. She paused, tapping her foot on the ground.

'But mama, how will I comprehend that he had the heart to leave me when I needed him most to survive how? If God had not sent my brother I would have been a dead person by now together with my child. For what reason does he wants to visit my child? He is a cruel man.'

'Yes, he is a coward and feels incapable of taking responsibility for being a parent but he wants to be called the father of a child. It is not the right attitude to have. In the white man's country, he would have been made to pay maintenance for you and the baby but here in our country we have not developed to that stage. Sometime, someday, it will happen. It will come.'

'What are you talking about mama,' inquired Yvonne. How can he take care of me when he has no love for me at all? I believe that if he had an atom of love for me, he would not have abandoned me the way he did.'

'It means that often boys are given the impression that the care and love of the children are women's duty while men move about.'

'Mama, you do not understand what my problem is. Love matters more than wealth. I cannot compare material things and love because love can survive without wealth but wealth cannot survive without love.'

'You are right. May be he thought you were desperate for him and so he pretended to love you while he sought only pleasure.'

'It is true mama, that idiot treated me as a thing to enjoy and drop. I regret now because I allowed it to happen. Yes, oppression exists when the oppressed allows it without resistance. Experience is the best teacher,' nodding her head.

She turned to Yvonne and looked into her eyes and saw her disappointment and disillusion and naivety. She said to her.

'Life is more mysterious than you can imagine. I am still learning new things everyday though I am your mother. Once beaten twice shy. So it will not be right to make another mistake by shutting him away from the child even if he has no love for both of you. It is good that he has an interest in the child. He has to contribute to his training.'

Yvonne bent her head in silent weeping.

'Mama, I don't really understand how, but I need time.' chimed Yvonne

'Take time but when you see him again do not be hard on him. Allow him to come to us so that things would be sorted out.'

Two months had drifted by before Ben appeared again this time in her work place. He must have found out from her friends where she worked. He was calm and wanted to speak with her outside the workshop. Yvonne ordered him to come back at five o'clock when they closed. Her heart was beating like someone who had run 400 hundred meters; she was not sure how to handle him.

Would she have the courage to face him? Her mother's advice flashed in her mind.

'So it will not be right to make another mistake by shutting him away from the child even if he has no love for both of you. It is good that he has interest in the child. He has to contribute to the training of the child.'

She knew that she would not miss this opportunity.

At five o'clock, Ben waited outside the workshop till she came to join him.

'Can we go to Thinkers Avenue and find a place in one of the drinking places to sit and talk?' asked Ben in a calm tone.

'Oh no we can talk here because I am in a hurry,' she said looking at Ben. He looked romantic and charming in his white shirt and black trousers, but she would not let that charm captivate her again. No, the line had been drawn and she needed to go straight to the point. Her mind flashed back to the day she was abandoned.

She had planted her eyes on the door as she sat on the chair inside the only room they shared hoping that he would turn up any moment. She had fought sleep like a lion to be awake to open the door for him. Then at midnight she had decided to take a risk and leave the door unlocked, but was then filled with fear and worry, and could not sleep. Her mind had travelled in circles like a clock until the morning and still there had not been any sign of him. Little did she know then that she had been abandoned when she was seven months pregnant.

Coming back to the present, her anger swelled up at his audacity to come demanding the child he had rejected three years ago. The voice of her mother kept interrupting her anger and pain. 'He must pay for the damage he has done.'

She started.

'Ben I know you came to ask for your child, well, you have to come and meet my parents to discuss it. My father is open to talking with you as far as the child is concerned,' she continued to move on while he followed behind.

'Ok but will your dad like to see me?'

'That is your problem now.'

'But you need …' he continued but Yvonne walked away.

He agreed to come but he did not tell her when. They parted in a strained and unfriendly way.

9

Ben's Family

Ben was taken aback by Yvonne's calm behaviour and response which was a direct contrast from what he experienced last time he met her on the street. He had thought it would take him more energy and time to get her to talk with him.

Ben was the only son in a family of five children. He was sent to one of the best government colleges in Mfoum Division. In some of the government colleges children were left free to roam the streets, as they liked. The teachers dared not scold or punish a child. That was because they were not sure whose son or daughter it was. If the child were a commissioner's child, a teacher could be jailed before they had time to defend their actions. At times parents threatened principals and teachers. The moral life was very low or non-existent. Children became unruly and could insult or even abuse the teachers. There were rumours that some parents gave bribes to teachers to upgrade their children and to make sure they did not repeat any class whether or not they passed. It was in that type of environment that Ben grew up until his father lost his job.

Ben dropped out of school and his mother was really worried about his behaviour but then he was too big and would not listen to her. He joined a gang of four boys who terrorised the neighbourhood. A few times he escaped being caught by the gardeners. His mother decided to send him to Furawa to his grandparents. There, he decided to join a group of motor boys in the car park. Motor boys were those who helped agencies to load cars and they were given tips but not much. He looked for odd jobs to occupy himself. At times, he was lucky and some other times he would go without a job for weeks. His grandparents were worried. Their suggestion to go and learn something like mechanics did not meet his approval. He wanted to join his uncle abroad but his uncle told him first to learn something so that he would be able to get a job abroad. With his half-baked education it was difficult for him to settle down.

He decided to learn and became a photographer. He had no studio. He seldom got jobs since he was not well established. He was still picking odd jobs here and there. It was on the day that he was covering a wedding as a photographer that he met Yvonne.

He was fascinated by Yvonne's laughter. She was also photogenic. His plan was to have her as his girlfriend. Yvonne persuaded him to seal the friendship by approaching her parents for marriage. He thought it was a nice idea but when Yvonne's father insulted him. He decided to drop the issue although Yvonne would not hear of it.

When Yvonne became pregnant, he was afraid that his parents would not accept Yvonne and the baby. He did not know how to tell Yvonne that he could not take care of the child. He ran back to Mfoum without letting his grandparents know the reason. He was not ready to father a child at that time.

He realized one day that he needed to tell someone about the relationship. The friend he confided in told him to go and get the child.

'Ben you look moody, what is wrong', one of his friends asked him.

He sighed. 'I have a child in Furawa.'

'Eh you are a father. You are a man now. Congratulations.'

'Do not congratulate me. I ran away from the girl when she was pregnant. I didn't know how to handle her and her pregnancy.'

'Is that why you came back from Bamenda? Go and get the child.'

'How?'

'How? The child is yours, you are a man. You have to establish your ownership before the girl makes up her mind and tells you that the child is not yours.'

'No, she cannot do that though that is possible because I have not seen the child since he was born.'

Laughing, his friend said, 'So you do not even know whether your child is a boy or a girl, black or white?'

'Oh he has to be black like me. I am not sure how I will take care of the child.'

'Ben, it is a great thing to be a father.'

That was when he approached Yvonne the first time and the second time he tried to be gentle. Yvonne told him to see her parents.

He finally decided that he must let his parents know.

Ben's father, Frank, had been the Bank Manager in Mesong-Mesala. Though modestly well-off, he was devoid of the kind of ambition that might have taken him much higher up his own particular ladder. The worst came when the bank crumbled due to bad management. Money had been loaned out to individual investors who made away with it and established themselves outside the country. The top managers and directors also invested some money into private business that did not yield any dividend to the bank. After a few years of struggling for survival, the bank had nothing to keep them going and so it was liquidated and in 1980 came to a final close. That was a source of some anguish to his wife Betty, who was very ambitious for her husband. She had worked hard on Frank for a great many years, urging him to apply for this and that job. Frank was a kind of carefree person who did not really bother so much about things or rather did not show that he was bothered.

When he lost his job as a bank manager, they moved to Mfoum and he became interested in gambling which took almost all the little money saved in his account. His gambling nearly tore the family apart. Betty implored his friends and family members to speak to him. He reduced the amount of money he spent on it but did not completely stop playing the fruitless game.

Ben went to the parlour but they were not there. They were sitting in the garden behind the terrace; it was an idyllic evening with a deep brilliant sky, the air full of birdsong. As he approached, he overheard his mother laughing at what his father must have said. One of his sisters was getting married and it seemed they were coming to the house in a few days' time.

He went and stood by his mother.

"Ben, you look worried; what have you been up to these days. You are hardly in the house. You have not told your father and me why you left your grandparents and came back here'.

Ben kept quiet and wondered how to begin.

'I ran into problems in Furawa,' he said.

'I thought as much,' said the mother. 'Now come out with it, what is the problem?'

'I… I have a child,' stammered Ben.

There was a long silence before his mother spoke.

'You have a child?'

106

'Yes mum, it was a mistake. I just wanted to be her friend and it happened.'

'Congratulations,' shouted his father. 'You have finished getting into trouble with police, now you are going about impregnating girls. That is your new job.' He got up quickly to hit Ben.

The mother stood between them and implored her husband to calm down. 'Let us get the details first. This would help to calm him down. He is already twenty eight years old,

'How do you know that the child is yours?' interrogated his mother.

'I met Yvonne at a wedding and we became friends. I went to see her parents and my proposal was turned down. She came and stayed with me. I love the girl and would like to marry her but I am not ready to take care of her and the child. I want to take the child but she wants me to see her parents.'

The mother looked at him and said,

'Ben, you cannot take the child without the mother because I am not ready to have children brought in here without a proper marriage. If you like the girl then you must be prepared to marry her and the two of you will build your home together. You have to grow up.'

'I have no job mum, and my mates are not married yet. I had wanted you and dad to go with me to assert the fact that the child is mine so that when he grows up he will then come to me.'

'One person cannot claim a child. The child is born by a father and a mother. It is cruel to remove the girl out of it and it will not help the child to grow properly. I completely oppose the idea of my son ill-treating a girl who had mothered his child.'

'Ben,' his father came in, 'you ran away before that child was born. You have not seen the child. You did not even ask the girl how she survived. You mentioned that her parents abandoned her and she stayed with you till you also left her. Now you tell us you love her but you do not want to marry her. You want the baby to be trained by her as your son. Why do you want to run away from responsibility? Now you go and reflect about it and tell us what you think. I'll give you a month to come up with your plan before we know what to do. Know that as far as you have not married her legally she and the child do not belong to you.'

'But dad the child always belongs to the man.'

'Only if they were married, now in this case you have planted in another's farm without consent. The seed would be lost if you did not settle with the farmer.'

Ben had sleepless nights wondering what to do. He had to get a permanent job. At the age of 28, he could not boast of any savings anywhere.

That night he dreamt and saw himself down in a pit filled with thorns and all kinds of dangerous weapons. He struggled to prevent himself from falling but a strong hand seemed to be pushing him down. He cried out from his sleep and woke up. He was afraid to go back to sleep again. He stayed awake for a long time before he could sleep again. The dream reoccurred and left him very weak and tired. His whole life looked a mess. He could still hear his mother saying

'You have to grow up,' and for the first time in his life he gave serious thought to his future.

He realized he had been playing the tortoise game. Now his whole life spread before him like a white sheet. There was no achievement in it. He had not completed his education and could not get a steady job. Here the saying holds good -

that when an old woman falls three times she must stop and count her belongings in her basket.

He wept in his room. He then remembered his camera; he had dumped it under his bed when he came back from Bamenda. He quietly bent down and dragged it out. He felt that he needed a change to his situation and to start again. His father had told him emphatically that he must make a decision about his life. He cleaned the camera and took it with him as he left the house.

It was a graduation day at the Nanga-Eboko university. Ben travelled all the way from Mboum to the University to take pictures. He took many pictures. One of the female students who posed for a snap resembled Yvonne. He was afraid to ask her who she was. When he washed the pictures, that one in particular stared him in the face. Could the girl be any relation of Yvonne? That picture made him think of Yvonne every day to the extent that it was a torture to his soul. That month he worked very hard and made some money. A friend helped him to get employed as a security guard at one of the colleges. He combined this with his work as a photographer.

At the end of the month, Ben realized that life was not judged by achievements but by the ability to wake up from a narrow view of life to a wider vision; to follow the right reason. He was going to follow his heart and not the selfish part of his make-up that wanted to hurt and conquer. He must grow up as his mother pointed out. He told his parents that he was ready to marry Yvonne.

His father inquired how he had come to that conclusion.

'Have you any means of maintaining a wife and a child? He asked.

'Yes he answered, and we will build our family together.'

He saw Yvonne as a key to his success in life and the way to make a difference in his life.

They went on to discuss on how to visit Yvonne's family.

Before they went, Ben had to find out if Yvonne would marry him. It was necessary to get in contact with Yvonne and ask her opinion. Was she ready to come back to him? He assured himself that his love would defeat hate.

Ben went back to Bamenda to see Yvonne. He met her after work. Yvonne knew that Ben was only interested in the child so she did not give him an audience. He could not risk following her to her house. He decided to write a letter and drop it with one of the apprentices at her work place. The next day Yvonne got the letter and read.

My dearest Yvonne,

I often wonder whether you can find any place in your heart to forgive me. I was foolish and naïve about how to love a woman. I was not ready to accept my responsibility for the relationship. When I came to ask for our child, I did not know what I was doing. I acted out of man's impulse to conquer, but now it is clear to me that I cannot do without you. I really love you and I am asking you to give me another chance to prove myself to you. I acknowledge that I have done wrong.

My parents and I want to come and see your parents if you approve. I will come to your work place in a week's time to see you. Please give me another chance to make it up to you.

Yours
Ben.

Yvonne read the letter again and again and decided that she would discuss it with her mother. She had a feeling that Ben wanted to play a game, although he had said that his parents were to come with him. Could it be part of their tactic or plan to get the child? She wondered.

'They will never take the child away from me.' She heard herself talking aloud. 'He never loved me, and he cannot possibly love the child. He has never taken me to his parents, so why are they coming?'

She decided that she would hide the letter and say nothing to anyone. She left the letter inside shirt she was wearing which belongs to Peter's. Unfortunately Peter discovered it.

10

Peter's Final Year

Peter's final year at the university came rather too quickly. The final examinations were tough as he had to combine his work as the president of the student's union with his studies. The election of his successor was deferred until after the examinations. He had to defend his course by producing 10,000 words on a topic of his choice. He worked hard and passed with flying colours. The graduation was fixed for August and he hoped that his family would be there to celebrate with him.

He planned to further his education with a Master's degree after graduation. He had been scanning the Internet for possible ways to do his Master's degree in criminal law abroad. He hoped to practice his profession as soon as he finished. He saw many openings and he applied to several Universities in the Sala Countries and the United States of America.

He travelled home to Furawa to wait for his graduation and to discuss his next move with his parents. Peter was a man with a great sense of purpose. That was one of the good things he had inherited from his father. His father was not particularly happy with his son's career. He had never supported him being a lawyer. He would have loved for him to have been a doctor or an engineer once the police force had been ruled out.

The journey took the whole night because of police checks along the way and the many bends on the road that the driver had to negotiate.

As a rule, one had to travel with an Identity Card. Everybody carried an ID card, but sometimes a tip of 500 francs could gain a person passage if they did not have an ID card or if they had forgotten it at home.

Some said that the only way to plead not guilty was to give a bribe.

'It is a corrupt system,' another man put in. 'What can we do?'

That type of experience often set Peter's mind thinking about his father. He was not sure whether he actually indulged in taking bribes in that way but as the saying goes 'One cannot swear for the child at one's back because he may have plucked the apple without the knowledge of the one carrying him.'

Peter had been kept awake many a night wondering why Ngong often referred to his father when he had problems. It was obvious that the police and people in the armed forces had a bad reputation in the country no matter how honest they appeared to be.

Peter gathered from one of his colleagues that many people regarded the military and the police as rogues who also supplied armed robbers with sophisticated ammunitions. Many seemed to choose to join the military because it was a lucrative profession and gave them an air of freedom. Sometimes, people believed that they had to bribe their way through to get qualified. Then they would be sent out on the road and made to collect money which would be shared with the directors who had assigned them the task. Allegedly, they were told how much cash they should bring in each day. If they did not bring in that amount they were fired. The most pitiable group was the women. Apart from collecting money for the directors, it was also asserted that they were abused by them.

Peter wondered if his father indulged in those acts. He had never brought anything home. He used to stand on the road though he would often come back early in the morning when they were still asleep or busy doing their morning duties. They were unconcerned about what he came back with. He always came home tired.

Now that he stayed in the office, could it be possible that he was among those who expected others to bring him a share of the money? If he did, where did the money go? He wondered.

He still believed that there were many honest people among them it was just that when one finger got soiled with oil it affected the rest.

It happened that Peter met Ngong on the bus to Furawa.

Peter's mind flashed back to the day he met him loitering at the park on his way home from work.

That had been about six years ago. Peter smiled and greeted Ngong,

'A great politician and potential future president,' and they locked hands.

'Oh Peter congratulations, I heard that you are a lawyer now. We will invite you to defend our case against the opposition party.'

'No, I have not arrived at the stage of defending great people like you,' Peter teased. 'One has to be above his wit to defend such an ostentatious group like yours. Now tell me, any hope for your party in this coming election?'

'Peter, you are talking as if you do not know what happened last week,' retorted Ngong. Then he continued sadly, 'The ruling party with their guns and money will never allow our head to crop up. We have no money to campaign and our Sala brothers do not want rivals. They hated us and blocked our progress. Did you not hear what happened in the North last month? It was a disaster.'

'I heard that the opposition party went there and fought with the villagers of the other party but I am not sure who fought who,' Peter chipped in.

'It was horrible Peter, do you know that our presidential candidate got drunk there. The other leaders wanted to smuggle him out of the scene unnoticed but he became very impulsive, insulted everybody. He ended up vomiting and messing up. Some rejected him as the president elect after the incident. The matter was made worse when a few members formed a new group from the party and decided to fight the existing party.

They elected another presidential candidate among them. Anger, commotion and fight sprang up and spread like wild fire. He laughed loudly; I had to run for my life.'

'Oh, so it was actually the same party fighting amongst themselves. 'A house divided against itself!' exclaimed Peter.

'Power hm, power rubs people of their senses. That was not all, continued Ngong. The villagers who came to listen and support us ran away. Tell me how they could vote for such a disorganized party. Peter, I have missed my opportunity in life. Look at you, a lawyer and I am still a pauper begging for my daily bread and answering Sir, Sir.'

'In fact what you described sounds like drama in a theatre. It reminds me of the misunderstanding between Brutus and Cassius in Julius Caesar.'

Ngong looked sad. 'I cannot remember why Julius Caesar was killed?'

'Marcus Brutus was Caesar's close friend and a Roman praetor. Brutus allowed himself to be cajoled into joining a group of conspiring senators because of a growing suspicion –implanted by Caius Cassius- that Caesar intended to turn republican Rome into a Monarchy under his own rule. In Act four, Brutus attacked Cassius for soiling the noble act of regicide by accepting bribes for the same reason Caesar was killed.'

'Yes, Brutus maintained his dignity, but in our party, everyone is corrupt.

One discovered all kinds of lies even the lies a devil will fear to tell in a group. Politicians know no friends, relations and no mercy as long as money is involved.

The craftier one has a better chance to succeed.'

'What is the point of being an opposition party, when the party cannot organize itself together for a common purpose?' questioned Peter.

'Peter, I desire now to do something different. I am tired of the whole system. I often remembered your words of wisdom and clear vision about making a difference in life.' He looked sad and resigned.

Peter asked him emphatically.

'What would you like to do?'

Ngong thought for a while and asked

'Can I go back to study at my age now? I did not even complete my A- level studies before I abandoned education. It looks difficult to go back.'

'It is never too late to learn and moreover there are other options like learning other trades or looking for jobs that may not need much education,' Peter pointed out.

Ngong was not happy with the suggestion of looking for work and he was no longer interested in the discussion. He switched off and went into his own thoughts.

'So, Peter thought he is the only one who can study. Now he wants me to get menial jobs for those who are not educated. I don't blame him.'

Peter wondered what was going on with him. He discovered that he suddenly became silent and was not willing to continue the discussion, so he kept quiet. The bus came to a stop in the park. They alighted from the vehicle and parted company. However, Peter felt sorry for him and wished he could still redeem himself as the saying goes to make haste while the sun shines.

Ngong was not happy that Peter had struggled and had finally achieved such a prestigious status while he had achieved nothing. Ngong did not want to meet him again because he posed a threat and presented himself as an achieved person or as a successful person on a pedestal which he, Ngong would never attain. He wondered what he would do next. He realized that their thoughts were never parallel and Peter always made him feel like a fool in a football field.

Peter arrived home early in the morning. His parents had not gone to work. Yvonne was in the kitchen preparing breakfast. The family was very happy to welcome Peter and congratulated him for his brilliant achievement.

'Oh I have a lawyer to defend my case now?' Yvonne said. 'Have you got a case to defend,' Peter asked smiling.

When they had all gone to their different places of work, Peter decided to arrange their rooms. While he was away from home, Yvonne had taken his room. He spent the whole day washing his and his sister's clothes. Yvonne had worn some of the shirts that he had left at home but he did not mind since they fitted her. He was humming a song he used to sing in secondary school when he felt a paper in one of the shirts. He removed the paper and opened the envelope. It was Yvonne's letter. He folded it back but an instinct urged him to open it and read. He argued that since it was his sister's letter, there was no harm in reading it. The letter was sent to Yvonne from Ben. He wondered who Ben was. He decided to find out from Yvonne when she returned from work.

He continued with his cleaning.

'How did that name fly into your mouth?' she was reluctant to talk about him. 'Anyway he is my ex-boyfriend.' grunted Yvonne

'Ex-boyfriend, the father of your son! Have you got a new one?' inquired Peter.

That is a closed chapter, snapped Yvonne, 'I no want do e thing with men any more. They are all deceivers like scarecrows.'

'Including me?' interjected Peter, surprised at her generalization.

'Oh no, you are my brother now and you are different.'

'Now tell me, has Ben ever visited you or written to you since you came back to the house?'

She ignored the question and her thoughts were like wild fire. She instantly remembered the letter and ran into the room looking for the shirt she had worn on the day she received it. She felt foolish for not having removed the letter from the shirt and hidden it. She did not find the shirt. She came out and asked Peter where it was.

'I asked you a question and you ran into the room, what is the problem?' cajoled Peter.

She kept quiet. She had no intention of disclosing anything about Ben or the letter to anyone. Obviously, she had not expected that anyone would dig into that matter again. She became upset with herself.

Then Peter quietly broke the hidden coconut and let the water out.

'Yvonne, I know you are looking for the letter sent to you by Ben,' mumbled Peter.

She turned to him. He continued without giving her a chance to talk.

'Yvonne you have every right to be angry and I support you in any step you have taken.'

Yvonne looked at him, 'I do not want to discuss him anymore.'

'He is a fool not to have thought of another chance for the past three years.'

'But he wants my child only,' retorted Yvonne. 'And he can never have access to him.'

'No, his letter to you said that he loves you but it is difficult to believe such tales. He must have been frustrated and wanted to try his luck again. However, the fact it took three years since the child was born, to appear makes me doubt that his love is genuine.' Yvonne's eyes were wet. She held on to her anger and pains.

'Peter you do not understand what I went through. It is difficult to forgive him.'

'I can remember vividly the situation when I found you. It is sad that he has such a heart to abandon a pregnant woman.'

'Yes, I have tried to forget my experience but it is not easy, I get flash-backs. It is difficult. I want to make him pay heavily before I let go, there is always a struggle within. My consolation is my son. I love my son.

'You know, in Europe a man would never abandon a woman and claim the child,' Peter explained.

'Peter, I will never allow it.'

Yvonne's son Gerald ran out of the room with new shoes calling, 'Mama, come and see my shoes, daddy brought shoes for me.' Gerald had been calling his grandfather, his daddy. 'Oh he is kind, did you say thank you to Daddy?' The child smiled and struggled to wear the shoes. Yvonne helped him and they all admired the shoes on his feet.

She wiped her tears and got up and went into her room, her child followed her. She went in search of the letter to destroy it but Peter had hidden it away and she did not want to talk about it again with Peter at that moment. She had to reflect on it alone before she could open the topic again.

Ben called Yvonne's work place one week after delivering the letter but she would not give him an audience. She silenced him but Ben was not easily defeated, and promised that he would give her time and come back when her anger had averted.

Kelly's result slip arrived by post that day and it was a happy moment for her. The family had double reasons to rejoice.

That weekend Peter and Kelly visited Sledge at the University in Nanga-Eboko. They boarded the night bus from Furawa and woke into the morning of the next day in Nanga-Eboko. Sledge was at the bus station to receive them.

11

Ben and Yvonne

Ben jerked straight upward in bed and stared wildly around. The clock on the table chimed 6 am. He opened his window, gave a confused shout and hurried to the bathroom. He brushed his teeth like lightning, splashed water quickly on his body and dressed in a flash. He had been day dreaming before he went to sleep and then he had overslept. It would be nothing but a miracle to meet the first bus. He planned to board the first bus to Furawa. He passed his mother at the door as he rushed out, muttered a greeting and told her that he was going to Furawa and would be back the next day.

'Will you not eat your breakfast before going?' inquired his mother.

'No mum, I am late. I will get something on the way.' He was half walking and half running as he answered. He flagged down a taxi and gave him an order to race or if possible to fly to the bus station. The driver smiled and set the engine in motion.

Luck was on his side, the bus was just about to depart. He wheezed and thanked his lucky stars. He would have been disappointed if he had missed the bus because he planned to meet Yvonne during her break to arrange the evening meeting. He felt it was not polite to surprise her as he had done in his earlier visits. If it did not work that day, he would see her the next day before returning to Mfoum. He settled himself on his seat and remembered that he had not informed his grandparents of his visit, so he got out his phone and dialled their number. His grandmother answered. She must have just woken up because her voice was not clear. He informed her that he was on his way and then switched off the phone. He was not used to phoning them to let them know when he was coming but she had asked him one day why he could not inform them that he was visiting. She would like to know of his coming in advance.

He sighed with relief and his thoughts came back to the present. He reflected on the best way to approach Yvonne. He realized that she was calmer than when he had met her outside her office. He decided that he needed to be there before twelve noon.

Yvonne came out with another apprentice chatting and laughing. His heart missed a beat but he knew he must act or he would lose the opportunity. He called out and greeted her and the colleague. Yvonne hesitated, tried to move on but thought better of it and stopped while the other person moved away from them.

'I do not mean to disturb your break time, could we arrange to meet after your work today, say at five o'clock?, asked Ben.

'What for? I thought we had decided on what you would do to see my son,' blathered Yvonne.

'Yes, but I would love to speak with you. There's more to it. Please give me another chance,' he pleaded.

'Another chance? Okay, I hope it will not be long,' warned Yvonne.

'No by no means, I will meet you here and then you can choose where we go.' Ben was thankful.

At five o'clock, Ben came as planned and they went together to one of the shops. Ben got some bottles of drink and they sat looking at the floor. Ben began by apologizing for his unruly behaviour.

124

'Yvonne, you have good reason to reject me and even to stop me from seeing our child because I have never seen him. I do not know what he looks like and I blame myself for that. But what prompted my visit is my burning desire to reunite with you again. I realized that my life is incomplete without you. I have been working hard and saving money to be able to bring you and our child home to create our family. Like a prodigal son I plead to be accepted back. I am ready to make amends if only I can be given a second chance. I love you more than ever. I have loved you all along but fear ruled my world of love then. I am ready to take the bull by the horns.'

Yvonne bent down and was fighting the urge to walk away and cry. The whole scene of what she had gone through flooded her mind. She burst out crying.

'Thank God for Peter, I could have been dead and forgotten by now.' She suddenly looked up and said stiffly,

'I was stung by the injustice of the whole encounter, how could you abandon me and the child in my womb, Ben? How could you? I gave you my love, my whole self and you used it and trashed it to the ground. All you told me was nothing but lies. How can I believe that it would not happen again? I am comfortable in my parents' house and I would not like to go through the experience again.'

Ben got up and knelt before her pleadingly.

'Please Yvonne, I am ready to repair the damage that is why I came back. It was not just the child that brought me back, but you. Many times I have cried even in my dreams. My parents are waiting for you. They long to see you. I long to make you mine, please Yvonne grant me this request. I will not fail you again, I promise.' He finished and fixed his eyes on hers.

She remembered her brother's words at this point. 'This could happen to anyone, give the guy another chance.' Then she looked at him and said,

'Ben, I have struggled to block out that name from my heart and I am on the verge. I know I had feelings for you before but not now. I find it hard to forget what has happened. However, you can visit with your family and we will see what might come of it. I am not making a promise because my father may not accept you. In the first place what jobs are you engaged in? How would you convince my father that you can take care of me and my child?

'Yvonne, I have been saving money since I went back to my parents. I continued my photography and I am also one of the gate keepers in one of the schools in Yaoundé. I am responsible now. Rather you have helped me to be responsible. I need to build my own family.'

'Well my dad will decide. He may not like all these jobs you mentioned.'

'But it is you Yvonne who will choose and not necessarily your dad. If you accept me, the job I do may not be a problem so long as I can care for you and our child.'

'I don't know, you did not communicate with me for three years, that is not a sign of caring, but you can bring your parents and we shall see what happens.'

'Oh thank you. Yes I did not call or come because I was still stupid. Thank you. It will be alright if we come next week, there is no time to waste. Talk to your parents and let me know, please.'

When they stood up to leave the shop, he handed her a bag. Yvonne had not noticed the bag before. She looked surprised. She enquired about its contents and Ben told her that it belonged to her and that she was free to find out. She took the bag and shuffled through its contents. There were all sorts of things ranging from creams, necklaces, ear rings, two pink blouses with a matching red skirt and pink high heeled shoes. She was surprised that he could still remember her favourite colour and shoe size. She thanked him and they moved out of the shop. He escorted her half way as Yvonne did not want him to come near her home. He went back to Yaoundé that night and informed his parents that Yvonne had accepted him back. His parents were happy and planned to pay a courtesy visit.

Meanwhile Yvonne discussed with her parents. Her father agreed that he would welcome Ben's parents and let them know how he felt and demand payment for the damage. Then they would clearly establish the fact that Ben had nothing to do with the child because they had never got married. However, the child could know about his father at the appropriate time. Yvonne revealed to her parents that she had sounded positive to Ben so that they would come and see them.

Yvonne sent a date and time to Ben giving them a month's interval when Joe would be on leave. Joe would not like to miss the chance.

12

Visits

Sledge was in her final year in the Accounting Department. She was thrilled with her brother and sister's visit. She shared all that had happened to her since she had enrolled at the University.

'I have to run from the lecture room to work ever since I registered to do this course. I have often wondered where I got the energy to do that and complete my assignments. The living conditions are not easy. You can see how small the room is and I am paying heavily for it.'

'I am very proud of you. You are already in your final year. The suffering will soon be over,' Peter added.

'I plan to go back to the insurance office and work as an accountant. I have already applied and I am waiting for the interview date to be announced. How is my little nephew? Is he walking and talking properly now?'

'Oh he has learned to play the tricks of children. When he wants to be cuddled he cries as if a snake has bitten him.' They laughed. 'He is three now.'

'I am sure you behaved like that too when you were small' Sledge came in.

'Oh all of us did in one-way or another. Everyone needs affection and love,' Peter responded and changed the conversation.

'I am planning to do my Masters outside the country. I will love to specialize in criminal law.' Peter said.

'I would have preferred you to have continued your studies here in this country,' Sledge said. 'I hear that

Nki'mbang is becoming a dangerous place, if the terrorists do not get at you, the youngsters who roam the streets will finish you with knives.'

'No, it isn't that bad. I spoke with Irene, my friend, the other day and she told me what was happening.' It is good to see what education is like outside the country as well. I will definitely come back to this country after my studies and put my talent to good use. In fact, I love my country with its green vegetation and natural arena that cannot be found elsewhere, more than Nki'mbang.'

'It is true,' sighed Sledge with relief.

'But how will you manage financially there?'

'If I have managed to pay my fees all these years in this country, then it will be possible anywhere. I am not a quitter. However, Dad has accepted to give me his bank statement for my visa interview next month.'

'Hm, how did you convince him, he does not seem to like you being a lawyer?

'Well I am already one, he has no choice.'

'Why do you prefer to do your Masters in criminology instead of moral or theological law?

'Why do you want to specialize in catching criminals though there are thousands of them in the country?' asked Sledge.

'Criminology means more than that.' Peter explained, 'the course is not so much about catching criminals but it is to do with moral conscience and right judgment.' He gave a detailed explanation and examples of what criminology means.

'The importance of fault in criminal law is reflected in the Latin maxim: *actus non facit reum nisi mens sit rea* (an act does not make a man guilty of a crime unless his mind be also guilty). This can be demonstrated through the following principles:

ACTUS REUS which means that the *actus reus* must be voluntary or freely willed for there to be liability.'

'That sounds good as it has something in connection with moral consciences.'

'I feel that you need to be attuned to your moral conscience as your life depends on the choices you make in life.'

'You know, at times I feel that you would have made a good priest if you had gone to the…'

'Do not be funny, I don't need to be a priest to live my life well. It is a call not just a choice.'

'For me every profession is a call and if you choose your own call, then you embrace it and thrive in it.'

'Yeah, you are right. You cannot thrive on the course you are not destined to do.'

'Congratulations Kelly! I heard you are planning to zoom to Nigeria?'

'It is still in the planning stage. I want to write the JAMB examination' (Joint Admission Matriculation Board Examination)

'Yes, I support the idea of you going over to Nigeria to study Theatre Arts because they are doing well in the drama factory and in fact, I think Nigerian movies have silenced or driven European films away especially in the African world. Kelly wants to specialize in art drama.'

'Do I need a visa to go to Nigeria?

'Yes, you need a passport and a visa because Nigeria is in the West of Africa while we are at the Central Region,' stated Peter.

'Oh, I hope it will not pose a problem for me. It is my great hope that in the near future all the African countries will have a common passport and we will be able to move around Africa freely just like in Europe and America.'

'That is our prayer,' came in Peter.

Sledge changed the topic and said,

'I read in the newspaper that some of the top army officials want to retire so as to be eligible to contest the coming presidential election. Our President does not want rivalry. The newspaper said that those top officials are not due or ready to retire.'

'We do not want an army regime in this country because we are a peaceful nation,' came in Kelly.

Peter looked at her and smiled.

'Do you think we are at peace in this country? The absence of physical war does not suggest the presence of peace. We are like a big pot boiling silently in the fire. People are afraid to quench the fire and clumsy to put down the boiling pot.'

'What do you mean by that?' asked Kelly.

'I mean that there are unaddressed problems in this country in every sector. Take for instance, the tax levy in this country. Everybody pays taxes whether they are working or not. People claim we learnt that from developed countries but in the Nki'mbang countries, only those who are working pay taxes and the government uses the taxes to feed those who are unemployed and the service users. They create job opportunities and put social services in place for the poor and the service users. People speak their mind freely without fear of being molested. Here, what infrastructure do we have to keep the young people busy or help the older people to enjoy their lives? You need to read current affairs, search the internet and observe what happens in other countries.'

'Dad wants to retire soon.'

'Why does he want to retire at this time,' asked Kelly.

'You know, dad is a masquerade that has no guide. He dances to his own music as he chooses,' replied Peter.

'You cannot believe that Felix came here to plead forgiveness.'

'What did you tell him?'

'Well I forgave him but the relationship is not possible. I have no feelings for him. He said that he was lured into abandoning me. It is like Mr Tom coming to ask for friendship.'

'Yeah, two of them seem to be in a similar category; low self-image and narrow minded.'

'When I remember those experiences, it makes me shudder. I recall the words of Jakes.' It says:

'There are people who can walk away from you. And hear me when I tell you this! When people can walk away from you: let them walk. I don't want you to try to talk another person into staying with you, loving you, calling you, caring about you, coming to see you, staying attached to you. I mean hang up the phone. When people can walk away from you let them walk. Your destiny is never tied to anybody that left. The Bible said that, they came out from us that it might be made manifest that they were not for us. For had they been of us, no doubt they would have continued with us.' [1 John 2:19] People leave you because they are not joined to you. And if they are not joined to you, you cannot make them stay. Let them go. And it does not mean that they are bad persons, it just means that their part in the story is over. And you have to know when people's part in your story is over so that you do not keep trying to raise the dead.

'The words are true to life. You cannot force someone to you. I mean it does not work.

In the story of the novel, Animal Farm, Napoleon and his satirical leadership confirmed this.'

He laughs. 'Apparently, Napoleon claimed to love animals while underneath, his plan was to turn them into slavery. Sometimes the human mind works in similar manner. The craftier you are the richer you become.'

'Jakes says: let them go. Do not try to raise the dead.'

'It all depends if you have the gift of faith and miracles.'

'Those gifts are reserved for God's favourites.'

'Oh I am definitely a favourite of God and if God sends the gifts to me, I would grab them in my two hands.' They laughed.

'I hope to join the insurance company when I my finish studies and do my best. I will then have the power to make choices and effect a change.'

'Remember, you cannot change someone who does not agree with your philosophy about life.'

'I know.'

They stayed with Sledge over the weekend and then went back to Furawa. Two months later Peter went to study abroad where Irene was.

Ben's family visited the family a month after Peter travelled to put across their request.

13

Ben's Parents Visit Joe's Family

en came with his parents to plead with Yvonne's parents and to make the necessary arrangements for the traditional wedding. They arrived in their car at 2.30 pm. They came with loads of gifts: 6 bottles of red and white wine, assorted cartons of beer and 5 crates of mineral water. It was a hot day. There was a hotchpotch breeze and heat which made it difficult to identify. The seemly warm atmosphere created a lot of heat and caused dresses to stick to bodies. It was the hottest part of the year.

The electric light had just gone off a few hours before they arrived and that made the heat worse. Joe was resting on a cushion placed in the garden when he heard the doorbell.

Yvonne welcomed them and let them into the parlour and informed them that her parents would join them soon. The little child ran out from the room and Ben controlled the urge to take the child in his arms. It was the first time he was seeing him.

Then his mother commented 'oh what a lovely child, can he be my grandson?'

Ben smiled and responded, 'Yes my son, look mum he resembles me, look at the mouth and the pointed nose.'

'You both wait first till we are received' said Frank.

'It is true,' agreed his wife.

Joe was called from his garden and his wife appeared and greeted their visitors. Joe looked straight at Frank without cordial greetings and asked as calmly as he could muster. 'Em what can I do for you?'

Frank cleared his throat and began,

'I am Ben's father and this is Betty my wife. Ben told us that he was friendly with your daughter for three years. Unfortunately, she became pregnant before my wife and I knew what happened. I must be honest with you, Ben did not tell us about this until a few months ago. I blamed him for that. We feel that a child must have a father and a mother and it is not proper to allow things to remain the way they are. We have come to ask your forgiveness for the wrong done to your daughter and to see how we can seal the relationship through the reunion of the two young people. The mistake has been made but it can be amended.'

'Thank you Mr Frank for your nice introduction. You mentioned that what your son did was wrong and you mentioned that for three years after it happened, you only heard about it a few months ago.'

'It is just to explain why we have not come since then,' interrupted Frank.

'Hold on, I have not finished,' Joe came in. 'Then you said it is not proper to keep things as they are now and you have come to seal the relationship. Well there has never been any relationship. What existed was exploitation and deceit. This created havoc in this family and not only that, it destroyed my child. It jeopardized my credibility in the neighbourhood. It was horrendous. It created more work for my wife and the entire family. So I wonder what you want to seal, your exploitation or deceit or more disgrace. Which of these have you come to seal?'

It was so quiet that you could hear a pin drop.

'Em, Mr Joe. Em, I do not know what to say. We come to acknowledge the fact that our son has done something wrong and he is ready to make amends. We ask you or rather we beg you and your family to find it in your hearts to forgive

136

him and accept us. We brought these drinks to ask for forgiveness. That is what we are saying. We are sorry that at times children follow their own minds and go beyond the acceptable norms in our society. I acknowledge the pains and difficulty your family went through alone and we would like to contribute as much as we can.'

'Mr Frank, you want to contribute to the irreparable damage your son caused to my daughter. Let me ask you, how would you restore or repair my daughter's virginity?'

'Ha, don't go that far please.'

'What! Joe stood up, what! You are telling me not to let out the truth. I warned that boy to get off my daughter when he came here, but he ignored me. I wondered how a nonentity like this could come to my house to bring shame and disgrace. If I were younger and full of energy, this story would have been told in the past. Thank your lucky stars. Now to cut a long story short, since you have identified yourself as the culprit, I would like you and your son to check the code of law and pay exactly what is demanded by the law for such a crime. That cannot even repay the damage done but it can help to train the child he forced into the world. That is all.'

'Please Mr Joe, we will pay whatever amount the law requires but would you allow these two young people to begin again? They have been seeing each other recently and have been talking. Give them another chance to be together.'

'I don't think I will admit such an irresponsible son as my son-in-law. Never will that happen in my family. Forget it and go home and train your son.'

Frank could no longer endure this and burst out.

'After all, this crime you talk about was committed by two people and not one. So allow them to build their life together.

If your daughter had been raised properly, she would have resisted my son.'

'So what are you doing here Frank? Leave this house before your corpse leaves here accompanied by your wife.' Joe got up again. Mary held him. Yvonne ran out to hold her father.

'Yvonne why are you out here? Did I invite you? Get out.'

'Your daughter is not the first person who has had this kind of experience. People have tried to make the best out of what they have but you seem to lack the patience to listen to reason.'

'Not until I receive the fine due to your son's crime. I heard that he had been harassing her on her way to work. I have informed the police to keep watch. So he is warned.'

'This is a mistake and …'

'Whether a mistake or misdeed, I do not want to set my eyes on him again. He did not pay a bride price to me, so I have nothing in common with you or your son. Again I say leave my house.'

Ben jumped from his seat and kneeling before Joe shouted-

'Please sir, I love her, I have loved her all the time but…'

'So you pretended to love her just to steal, and you abandoned her to die.'

'No Sir, it was a mistake. I was naïve and afraid of how to cope with the situation when she became pregnant. I had no job or means to keep her. But now I have got jobs. I can care for her and our child. Please Sir, give me a second chance.'

The weather was cool. The hot sun had passed by and ushered in a gentle breeze. Ben knelt and waited for his response; a word or something to calm his tumbling heart. It seemed ages before Joe spoke in a calm voice.

'I am glad you spoke young man because you are the main actor in this story of destruction. Tell me what job you are doing with your half-baked education. Convince me of how you will feed my daughter and her son. What would prove to me that you will not abandon her in the future?'

Silence prevailed for a while. Ben looked at his parents, breathed heavily and picked his words carefully.

'Sir, I am really ashamed of myself and my past behaviour. You have a right to be angry and treat me the way you desire. It is true I left Yvonne in a very vulnerable situation. I have thought of my actions and have approached her several times asking for forgiveness. I went back to Yaoundé and got a security job. I also take photos. I have prepared a place where Yvonne and I can build our home.'

'Good, and which company do you work for as a security man?'

Ben looked down, 'I am a gate man in one of the primary schools.'

Joe laughed sardonically, 'how much do you earn in a month.'

'Mr Joe, I think what matters is to accept him first and other details will come later because this interrogation is too much,' Frank burst out.

'Have you heard the saying, 'faith without good work is dead?' This implies that love without material wealth to support is dead. You cannot feed my daughter on empty promises and the few miserable francs you receive.'

'I promise to do my best Sir, give me another chance.'

'Well, I have heard all your sermons. You have to go for now and give us time to think over it, then I will come back to you if necessary, but make sure that you pay the compensation amount within two months or we will meet in court.'

'Frank let us go, and you Ben get up,' came in Betty.

' please sir give me the chance to amend my mistake. I love Yvonne,' added Ben.

As they moved out, Joe asked them to carry their drinks with them. When they left Joe continued talking.

'Imagine the man telling me that the crime is committed by two people. I could have dragged them to court so that by the time they finish with the payment of a lawyer, they will know that it is not an easy road.'

'But you were too angry,' pointed out Mary.

'When I look at the boy and remember how I warned him before this happened I get very angry. Foolish boy, doing a security job for a living, how much does he earn in a month? Looking at him he is too poor to care for my daughter. He cannot feed himself with whatever he earns.'

'True, I am not really sure how he will take care of a wife with the kind of job he is doing,' Mary added.

'That is the point. How will you know what he is up to? I do not understand that family.'

'What about them?'

'They are a very pompous family. It is surprising that they come to ask for forgiveness without claiming the child. I thought they would talk about the child, and then I would vomit my venom…Time will tell.'

'What do you mean by that?'

'Yvonne is not going anywhere for now.'

'I know but when are we going to give them a response on where we stand?'

'I am not obliged to declare my stand to anybody about my own daughter.'

'I know, but she needs to live her life.'

'Woman, we leave this for now,'

Yvonne came in, 'Dad please forgive them.'

'Who invited you into this discussion?'

'Dad, this is about my life, I am old enough to participate when my future is being discussed. I like him.'

Joe looked at her annoyed. 'You have come again. What do you know about love? You are not mature enough to be in a relationship with that boy who abandoned you and left you to die.'

'But dad, I am…'

'That chapter is closed for now.'

Joe did not wish to continue and he left the room.

'Mum, it feels weird and sad the way dad treats me in this house. He does not listen to my feelings or my opinion.'

'Well it is a difficult situation because a mistake has already been made.'

'Yes, I know but we can give him a chance.'

'We will talk about it later.'

'Do you know what? I feel that dad does not want me to get married like most fathers do in this country.'

'He cannot marry you, he is thinking of your own good.'

'I have the feeling that he has another woman somewhere; what does he do with his salary?'

'You are jumping from one thing to another. We will talk about it later, you are angry now.'

'Yes, I am and why can I not speak about my pains and disappointment?'

'Your dad will not listen now. I will talk with him later. Leave it at that for now.'

The next day, Yvonne shared her disappointments with Eileen. She went to see Eileen during break.

'Do you mean to say that Ben came to ask for forgiveness and seek your hand in marriage and you refused? Do you not love him anymore?'

'Eileen, it is not that, I would love to forgive him but my father adamantly refused to listen to emotional needs and centred his refusal on Ben's poor salary and uncertainty to feed a new family. I would like to get back to him. His financial status has improved as he told me a few weeks ago. I would like to get married to him but my father would not hear of it.'

'You have the right to choose who to marry. It is your future, it is your life. Your father is not going to live with you.'

'I know but it's just that I disobeyed him once and now I do not have the courage to disregard his decision again. I may ebb away and remain single all my life. I feel trapped.'

'Speak to your mum.'

'My mum promised to speak to my Father. I wish I had a particular ability or quality that Peter and Sledge have to follow their hearts. Peter became what he wanted despite my father's neglect and idolized urge to force him to join the Military. Sledge finished her studies without my father's assistance but here I am under his command of unforgiving heart.'

'A pursuit of happiness is the chase of a lifetime! It is never too late to become what you want to be.'

'I do not have a strong will to carry out my plan. I hate myself for my inability to follow my heart in this particular issue. I feel my whole world will crumble if I disobey my father. My future is filled with gloom and I am sad.'

'Why should parents especially your father decides whom you would marry? It is very unjust; I mean it is not allowed in the 21th century. This has been the trend of attitude towards some of my friends too. Some parents remain locked in their out dated minds and abusive culture; culture that robs women of the power to make a choice of life and use their freedom.

feel sad when I listen to experiences like yours. And your dad is educated,' Eileen went on. 'Education helps to affect a change on peoples' behaviour and ways of thinking but in this particular case, education finds it hard to challenge injustice.'

'I feel bad but I cannot withstand it if my father rejects me.'

'I suppose that is another issue. Everyone needs the blessings of their parents. Come to think of it now what if one chooses justice rather than obedience that jeopardizes one's future happiness?'

'The issue is how to know what future will bring if I disobey my father and get married to Ben. I will be alone in that case. My father can go a long way to make things hard for me.'

'But I think that if one fights for a clear and just cause, God will see him through.'

'Eileen, I do not have such faith. I want to go back to my work. Thank you for sharing your thoughts with me.'

'Take care.'

14

Sledge Faces Challenges

Sledge wrote her final examination and passed with flying colours. Her family rejoiced with her. She got a job as a clerk in the social insurance department three months after her graduation. Eight months later, she was transferred to the North-West. She was happy to move back to the Bamenda Branch.

The social insurance is a government run company that offers social services in the following areas: pension, family allowance and child care. The three areas each have their own separate office and Sledge worked in the pensions department.

The first thing Sledge did was to re-arrange her office. She retrieved all the old files from the filing cabinets and sorted them out. Some of the files had been there for years and the owners had either died or got tired of chasing them and had given up. She selected the most recent files and brought them to her table.

Sledge recognized some of the names and saw that sadly some of them had died without getting their pension. She could do nothing but refile them neatly away. She hoped to inquire about the files that had come in between ten years to five years and nursed the hope that the owners would re-appear again for them. There were some that were still recent which she prepared and sent to Yaoundé. There were many unattended files and she needed to create extra time to attend to them. More files continued to pour onto her table. She made sure that those files had all the required documents before she sent them to the director for approval and for forwarding to Yaoundé.

Sledge believed that those who had worked for the nation and had paid taxes deserved to be cared for by the government when they retired. It was a crime to neglect people like that.

There was a case of a teacher who had been retired for the past ten years. He had filed his documents several times to the pension department but whoever was there had done nothing to forward his file. He got tired of sending documents as they continued to demand more from him. He had decided to sue the social insurance company in court and demand his full pay but the director feigned ignorance of the case. Sledge wondered how long it could be kept under water before it erupted.

There were a number of vulnerable people who had no one to speak for them. The system of payment was disorganized and it remained a big issue as it took weeks every month to pay the service users.

Sledge had a visitor. She could not recognize the visitor but her mind kept wondering where she had met him before. The man spoke:

'When I heard that you were back in social insurance and that you were closer to me, I decided to come and see you. You may have forgotten me but I will never forget what you did for me in Eklewindi.'

'Oh?'

'Yes, you may not know many people you helped to live on in Eklewindi.'

'Do you still go to Buea to receive your pension?'

'No, I no longer go there to receive my pension, I receive it in Kumbo.'

'Oh Papa, I am glad to hear about it and how are you keeping?'

'I am well but something else brought me here. You are what we need in our country. A heart without corruption is a special gift. My son has the same problem I had. He was a primary school teacher and resigned because what they paid him as a teacher was never enough to maintain his family. He decided to start his own business. The local government tax is too much. My son thought that he would get his pension to augment his income but for the past years, there has been nothing. He wanted to take the social insurance department to court but a poor man cannot fight the government and moreover he cannot get a lawyer to defend him.'

'Has he filed the case in court? I saw a file in connection to that.'

'His name is David.'

'Yes, that is the name. Papa, will you ask your son to come and see me? He may not need to go to court.'

'That is why I came to see you. I am happy that they have not pushed you away completely.'

A week later David came to see Sledge. They traced his files together and Sledge told him 'the problem is not with the social insurance department but with some workers who have no conscience because if your file is not forwarded for signing, there is no way it will get through. Some workers are nonchalant.'

A few weeks after that, David started receiving his pension. Sledge helped many people to smile and to realize that it was not the government that was the problem but those who worked for it.

Sledge was promoted three years after she resumed work; she was promoted to Assistant Manager. Six month later her manager was sent to Mpongo and Sledge was asked to fill the gap of the manager in the social insurance department. She was to cover the Northern part of the country as far as Furawa and beyond.

Sledge tried to observe the other Managers and discuss with them informally about the problems and issues that affected the public. She tactfully realized that there were some Managers who would behave like the man who sacked her a few years ago in Mpongo. She knew she must be cautious or she would spoil her long term plan of rebuilding the social insurance department and jettisoning the ghost workers and those who demanded bribes from the vulnerable public. The difficult part was that some of the managers and directors were involved in the crime. It was a difficult situation.

However, people began to notice that their family allowance was being paid promptly and everyone was attended to without too much delay. People wished that other departments would be the same. She gave incentives to the workers from time to time to motivate them and to make sure that they were not disgruntled in their work.

Sledge faced a stranger one morning in her office.

'I know you from the past history. You worked in Mpongo for a few years past and caused the insurance department problems that took them time and money to ratify. How did you become the manager in the North-West?'

Sledge listened silently.

'You are the one who claimed to discover ghost workers in the company. Did you know that many managers and other workers lost their jobs on account of your fury? Now you are here doing the same thing.'

'Who are you? And how can I help you?'

'It is not important but let me warn you, there is no way we can allow you to continue like this.'

148

'If you are not a coward get straight to the point. What do you want?'

'Good, you are a very intelligent lady. I was sent by one Mr Tom. He was not sure whether you were the same Sledge that worked under him.'

'Oh I see,' Sledge laughed. 'How is he? Send my regards to him.'

The stranger was shocked at the manner Sledge took the threat.

'Well I was asked to find out who the manager of this well performing department was. Mr Tom will be shocked to know that you are manager now.'

It was then that Sledge recognized the face.

'Mr Jude, yes, you are a friend of Mr Tom's. You came to find out for your friend what is happening in the North-West. Well, tell Mr Tom what you have discovered and wish him well. Good day.' Jude left her office. Sledge dismissed the visitor with a sigh.

15

Peter In Nki'Mbang

Peter was happy to reunite with his friend Irene. The first thing that impressed him was the city of Nki'Mbang. It was magnificent and well planned; houses, roads, recreational centres, museums, beautiful bridges especially the Special Bridge were master pieces. In fact, there were many beautiful sites that could leave your mouth open for hours. Irene told him that each county was organized in such a way that no particular area lacked any thing. The same shops were in the entire county. The social services were well arranged. The transport and health services were superb; the elderly and children were all catered for.

Peter's experiences were mixed with surprises and challenges. Back at home, people believed that all Nki'mbang countries had risen above human suffering that they were very rich that people could pluck money from trees. Many people believed that once you were able to cross over to Sala areas, your problem of poverty and needs were over, and then you were expected to keep sending money to those in Africa. A distorted picture of Nki'mbang was presented at home and it was hard for those who struggle to survival to return home when they could not manage. It was unbelievable to listen to news and read in the newspapers about three thousand people who had no jobs in Sala and Nki'mbang countries. It was disheartening to learn about thousands of children who slept in the streets especially at hidden places in the main cities. Unfortunately, you could be attacked by the younkers moving around with knives.

However, Peter was challenged by the activities of police and shared with Irene his small findings.

'I am impressed with the work of the Police Force here. The crime rates were drastically reduced compared to my country. Being a capitalist nation the Government practically controlled peoples' lives. They collect taxes from the employed and take care of the jobless, the vulnerable and service users. And yet different kinds of abuses go on in the country.' He paused and continued,

'I am surprised to hear from the news that some parents abuse their children here despite all the warnings and laws guarding against it,' Peter said.

'Oh the situation is hard,' Irene responded. 'One hears of homicide, people killing either their partners or children; fathers raping their daughters or step daughters. People abandon their partners on the slightest misunderstanding. The divorce rates seem high and many people are not interested in marriage. There was a story of a man who raped his two daughters more than eight times over ten years and they have four surviving children from him.'

'When there is denial for needs of moral conscience, such things take root. How was he given custody of the children instead of the wife?'

'It is difficult to tell. Their father threatened them so they could not report their predicament to anyone. The social workers were blamed partly because they did not listen to the children when they complained though it was not clear where they reported the case.'

'You see, the police tried to trace these crimes and bring the people to justice.'

'There is a lot of work to do. Many people are not happy and yet the government provides everything for them.'

'No, the Government does not see the point. When they provide everything for its people without giving space to sweating for it, it does not work out well. Hard times seem a good technique for sharp thinking, planning and hard work.'

'You may be right there considering the fact that the young girls who get pregnant out of wed lock are provided with houses to live and childcare benefits from the government. So why would they not get pregnant every year,' Irene sighed.

'Eh, is it how things are done here?

'Yes, and the more children they produce, the more benefits they receive from the government. Then they have no reason to make an effort to work or to pin down the boys responsible for the pregnancy. Many of them are drop outs. They cannot study too.'

'That is why there are lots of single parents; many not interested in marriage anymore.'

'One of my course mates cries every night. Her parents separated and moved on with other partners. She is left on her own to work and manage her life. She finds it difficult to keep friends on a long term basis. She does not know what to do. Luckily, she goes to counselling but she does not know how to win her parents' love back. Tell me how such a girl will ever settle with anyone. She cannot give what she does not have.'

'Well the upbringing is different here. Though my parents did not educate me they are always there for me. You feel the love and you have a base. You have a place you call home, but here in Nki'mbang, home means different things for different people.'

'Peter, honestly I do not really understand how someone from a warm African continent would like to stay here. Education is wonderful but I feel that if we have sense we should go home and improve our country and our educational system.'

'I cannot wait to finish my course. I love my discipline and the guys there are just wonderful and friendly but home is the best.'

Three months later, Peter got a call from Asong, his friend and colleague from Eklewindi.

'My brother, please don't forget me in your kingdom. I have tried several times to get a visa to Europe but it has proved impossible. I believe that if I struggle and come over there, things will be better.'

'Well, it is not easy to get a visa and often the criterion for getting a visa is not clear. If you apply to study, the university will send a letter that might facilitate the visa.'

'Please I need some help. You know how difficult it is to get a job here.'

'The struggle is the same at home. I managed to get a part-time job that barely paid enough to clear my fees and accommodation.'

Peter don't tell me you are crying as well. Man, you are in Europe. You can even see a job to apply for. I know you are fine. Please do something for me now. At least 200 quid will keep me on. We are friends.'

'There is no way you could understand how it is in Europe unless you came. My school fees is 10 thousand Euro (€10,000) and my accommodation fee for a year is two thousand seven hundred and fifty Euro (€ 2,750). I earn four hundred Euro every month. I have to eat, buy books and pay my transport.'

'Oh my God, where would you get such an amount of money?'

'I was lucky to get a job as soon as I got my national Insurance Identity card. It takes months to get a job. Do you know that I travel from lecture to where I work? I go to lecture during the day and then work at night just to make ends meet.'

'So when do you study then?'

'You study in-between times and you must clear all your assignments. In my class, we have paper presentations every week. We are divided into small groups of seven. Each group must present 5,000 critical analyses on a given topic.'

'Oh I thought you were swimming in milk and honey.'

'As I said earlier, you cannot understand how life is here. We complain about taxes at home, but here you pay taxes for everything. You cannot watch television here without paying taxes even as a student. It is simply living from hand to mouth because you have to clear your bills including income tax, electricity bills, and phone bills.'

'But you pay tax when you buy items at home.'

'It is nothing compared to what we pay here. I suppose they have not known any other life to compare, so they feel life here is the best.'

'Of course it is the best you cannot convince me Peter that things are hard there. I heard that education is free for the home students.'

'No, it is not true. The Government gives loans to students though it makes some of them lazy. They pay back when they finish and get jobs. They give them an allowance which serves as pocket money. You would be surprised to hear that some youngsters here do not attend school. The government provides for service users and the jobless. I love the idea of caring for the less privileged.'

'We do help the poor through the social insurance services. Do not forget that people receive pension after they retire.'

'Yes it is true, our government is doing the best they can in their situation but the difference from our system is that in addition to pensions and other benefits, the Nki'Mbang government also feeds the jobless and the less privileged. I am hopeful that we will rise one day to helping those who have no work or pension.'

'Peter' thanks for this information. I think I will give up applying for the visa and try to establish myself here since the world is the same. If I will have to struggle when I come to Europe then I rather stay here.'

'It is good to travel, see the other side of the world and it is a good idea to return home after your expeditions. I am leaving this country as soon as I finish my studies. I believe that home is where I will make a mark and not here. We need to rebuild our country and then improve the standard of living.'

'So you are coming back next year. If you had not explained to me how you were struggling there I would think you were mad for wanting to come home.'

'You see, Africa gets under your skin whether your experience is pleasant or not you are left with a tingling desire to return perhaps it's an ancestral echo calling us to the evolutionary cradle of human kind but perhaps the appeal is simpler and a more visceral life overflows there filled with joy and an air of freedom, generosity beside violence; wealth overlaid on poverty; hearty warmth and volatile passion, unfettered by any agreed code of etiquette. It is weird that Africans choose to remain in Nki'mbang and Sala countries when they finish their studies. I mean I am happy with the experiences I gained but I prefer to return home and contribute my ideas to the development of our nation. I mean, the quality of education here is good. At the same time our educational system could be upgraded if we were disciplined and forgot nepotism and tribalism syndrome.'

'That is a big issue. Most of our best brains remain abroad after their studies. Peter, I do not blame them completely because our government does not acknowledge their gifts.'

'That may be true but the reality is that those who want to challenge the system are silenced with the gun.' The truth is, it continues to struggle with endemic corruption, an exploding population, environmental pollution, militancy, and tribal violence. We are a Nation with kaleidoscopic colour and diversity, warm personalities, and a bustling energy.'

'We will rise one day. How is your sister, Sledge?'

'Oh she is the manager at the social insurance company. She is doing fine. Thank you for your call. If you are on Skype we can communicate often.'

'I will try to down load it but we can only use it if there is light.'

'That is another point, you know that light never goes off here.'

'Until recently we had stable supply of electricity. I do not know what has gone wrong.'

'That is our country. There is hope. We will get there; it took Europe about 600 years to get to where they are. Slow and steady we will get there.'

'Invariably, we learn only from experiences and our suffering.'

'It is unfortunate. Thank you for calling.'

'You are welcome.'

Peter realized that the University he chose was one of the prestigious institutions in Nki'mbang. There were 116 candidates registered for MA in criminology, out of that number 80 people came from different countries of the world.

Peter found it challenging and at the same time filled with admiration for the Nki'mbang government that provides allowances to their home students and also gives them loans to continue their education. Some students use it well, while others drink it away and live care-free lives. Peter was sad that the African continent could not build their countries up.

'We have all the resources we need to establish ourselves in all ramifications and yet, we find it hard to start. I know what we need, yes, a change of attitude and less greed.'

Peter did well in his studies. He had to submit a dissertation of 20,000 words for Master's work. He gained a lot of experiences both in the academic and experiential aspect of the course. Peter was happy with his achievement and he was happy that he listened to his inner desire to study criminology. He planned to call home next week to inform his family about his success and his home coming.

Irene also finished but wished to practice her nursing for few years before returning home. Her parents lived in Wales, and so she visited them from time to time. She would have loved to return home but her parents insisted that she stay for a while.

16

A Sudden Disaster

The weather was gloomy and wore a sad look. Yvonne arrived home from break on Monday morning and found her mother in tears.

'Mum why are you crying? What happened?'

'It is your father. I just got a phone call.'

'A call from him?'

'Major Ibrahim called to say that they have had an accident and things are bad.'

'Mum let us go to the office. I will accompany you.'

'It has just happened and they have called the police to register the incident.'

Yvonne called Sledge immediately and they went to Joe's office. They met Major Ibrahim and a number of army officials when they arrived. Mary directed her questions to Major Ibrahim.

'Where is he? What happened?'

Major said nothing and led them to Joe's office. The remains of Joe lay motionlessly in his pool of blood. The police had taken pictures and noted other necessary things like the foot and finger prints. The ambulance stood at the entrance of Joe's office. The two gate men had been questioned. They alleged that they did not see any one entering Joe's office but they heard a gunshot a few minutes after Mr Joe had come down to the gate and spoken to Remand, one of the security guards. One of them confessed that he saw the back of a man in black shirt and black trousers as he jumped the fence but that was immediately after the gun shot was heard. Joe's office was closest to the gate from the main entrance. Remand went up to look and saw that Joe laid face downward. He shouted and others ran to the scene of the accident. They called Major Ibrahim immediately. An emergency call was made to the police station and the hospital.

'Who could have done this.' asked Yvonne half shouting to the policemen and half directed to Mr Ibrahim.

Mary's mind flashed back to the discussion she had had with Joe two weeks before.

It was when they had finished their supper and relaxed in the parlour watching television. Joe stated casually.

'There are commotions at the barrack because the presidential election is coming soon. The rumour in the air is that some high officials in the army want a change of government. They want to retire in order to contest for presidency during election. Actually, I would like to retire for I have served the nation for 35years. But some of the directors are against it and are suspicious of the idea of my retirement. Those who are due to retire did not want to retire. So there is confusion among the generals as to who wants to do what.'

'But why not wait for this period to pass by before you retire. The election is next year. You can tender your resignation after the presidential election,' Mary suggested.

'But anybody who suspects me must be out of his mind. I cannot rule this country now because it is in a real mess. I am not ready for that hassle. I need to retire and enjoy the rest of my life. You know I entered the army at the age of 18. I have been in the service for almost forty years. I need to give the young ones a chance.'

'I know but what I am saying is to first allow this confusion of retiring to pass, so that you won't create

160

suspense and jealousy. Moreover, you are not yet sixty years old.'

'No, I have already written to the head quarter and I am waiting for a reply.'

Mary cried bitterly. 'That is it.'

The police were there measuring and struggling to make meaning of the situation and how the person or persons were able to escape from the barracks unnoticed. It seemed to be a planned assassination as they have ruled suicide out.

'No, Joe is not a man to take his own life,' confirmed Major Ibrahim.

At round five o'clock on the day of the murder, two police guards had just handed over to the next shift. Joe had been seen by the four police men because he came to the gate and spoke with Remand, one of the guards and then went back to his office. Not long after that, a gunshot was heard. It was not clear whether the person sneaked into his office and waited for him to return from the gate or followed him in as soon as he came back from the gate. It was difficult to establish how it happened. No traces were seen but an unusual disorganization of window curtains and traces of foot prints were discovered. A search was made and it was discovered that the window had been forced open. There were no scratches or bruises on his body, except for the spot on his neck where the bullet hit him. From all indication, he died instantly.

As they stood at the door of his office, a woman came in yelling and rolling on the floor uncontrollably. One of the police officers turned and asked if she were the wife. Major Ibrahim answered him, 'No the wife is standing beside me with her children.'

The police officer went and told the woman to get up. While they helped her sit up, she kept shouting,

'My life has come to an end, I am finished, Joe why? How will I manage with the children?'

At that stage everybody was asked to leave the office so as to give room to arrange the remains to be conveyed to the mortuary.

The police took the details and confirmed the incident a murder case.

'Who is that woman mum,' queried Yvonne.

'I have no clue; I have never seen her or heard about her.'

That night Peter called to let his family know that he had submitted his thesis and hoped to return home in two months' time.

Sledge answered the call.

'Peter, darkness has fallen over us during the day.'

'What do you mean by that, I hope everyone is fine.'

'All is not fine. Dad is no more.'

'What do you mean by that?'

'He was assassinated in his office. We are just coming back from the barrack. Peter, it is a horrible thing. I was about to call you when you called us.'

'Who killed my dad and for what reason?'

'I heard it was political.'

'Political, how? Papa was never interested in politics. What happened exactly?'

'I cannot tell you now. The police have taken statements and noted the incident as a murder case. It must be followed up. Peter, please come home,' she broke down in tears. Their mother picked the phone,

'Peter darkness has covered the light. Your dad was killed by assassins.'

'Mum is it true? No, mum I am coming home. I will call when I have booked my flight.'

'Ok my son,' the burial may not be immediate since it is a murder case. I will discuss with major Ibrahim and your uncle to learn the procedure.'

Two days before the burial, the same woman who appeared in Joe's office came accompanied by two young girls. She was dressed in complete black. Her hair was dishevelled. She walked straight to where Mary sat on a mat at the corridor.

'Madam, I am sad that this has happened to us.'

Mary looked up and into her face.

'Us? Who is us? Who are you?'

'I mean you, me and our children. I have five children with Joe and he had been a very good and supportive father to his children especially in their education. He promised to train them to the university level but now his sudden death has created a vacuum,' she burst into tears.

Mary was confused and she kept looking straight into thin air. Yvonne came along at that stage.

'Mum what is happening here? Who is this woman?' No one spoke.

'Get up madam.' Yvonne said almost shouting. 'What do you want?'

Sledge ran out from the room and held Yvonne.

'Yvonne wait, we must not create a scene on our father's burial.' Sledge greeted the woman gently and asked,

'What can we do for you madam?'

The woman looked up at Sledge and asked,

'Please are you Joe's first daughter?'

'It does not really matter for now, what can I do for you?'

'Ok I am Joe's wife. I have five children from him and he had been educating and supporting them all these years. So I came to make myself known to his traditional family.'

163

'Ok you and my dad had an affair and you feel you are part of his life. Good, now get up let me show you where to sit for now. You cannot sit together with my mum because we have only just learned about you today. We need to investigate your story.'

'Which story interrupted Yvonne? There is no story to investigate. She is an intruder.'

'No Yvonne, we will find out soon. It is ok for now.'

The woman got up and followed Sledge. She was shown a cushion in the parlour. She sat there with her children.

Peter came home that day and did his own bit of crying though he had cried when he disclosed the news of his father's death to his friends.

'Peter, there is another delicate problem which we must handle carefully,' explained Sledge.

'Look at that woman sitting there with her children.' Sledge pointed with her eyes.

'She claims to be the second wife of Joe. She said she had five children by our dad and he had been supporting and educating the children till late. She was there at the office when we first heard the news. No one is sure about her story but we must be careful. Let the burial be done and then we will look into her case.'

'What is the meaning of this? What type of story is this?'

'She must not be allowed to take part in anything. I don't believe that woman at all. She has to leave this compound,' splattered in Yvonne.

'Wait;, did the woman say that she got married to our father or what? And mum did not know about her.'

'Mum said she has never heard about her till now. That's why I feel she is an intruder,' Yvonne insisted.

'Ok this is no time for this kind of news. Let's look at the burial plans. Where is uncle?'

Their uncle came in at this stage and they told him about the woman.

'No we have to establish something first.' He went to the woman.

'Hello madam my name is Kingsly, a brother to Joe. I don't seem to know you.'

'Oh hello Mr Kingsly, I am Angel. I have been the biological wife of your brother for 15 years. I have an obligation to fulfil at Joe's burial. I feel sad that he did not introduce me to the members of his family before his untimely death.'

'As you rightly said, we were unaware of the fact that my brother had children outside the marriage. I feel that it is an issue to discuss after the burial as we would not like an uncomfortable scene to be created at this painful time. I implore you to remain calm and unnoticed till this period is over and then we will talk.'

'To remain unnoticed? No, I think this is the right time to make myself known. I am tired of being in the background. That is why I came with my children who also missed their father. How can you ask me to remain unnoticed? It is not possible now. I thought you would understand better than the children.'

'Excuse me madam, I mean to say that we cannot introduce you here as Joe's wife because we do not know about you. We need to investigate your story.'

'Well, if you want to postpone the burial and investigate my story first, I am ready, but not to be part of this final farewell to Joe will be difficult. He was also my husband.'

'Ok what do you want to do for Joe?'

'Good, I want to join the family in giving him a befitting burial. I am his second wife.'

'No, this does not sound right. My brother did not tell me about his second marriage and therefore, we cannot accept your story just like that.'

'You better listen to me now because my children have a share in Joe's property and things. I will take it wherever it will stretch to establish my position in this matter.'

'As I said this is not the right time to do this. Please can you be patient with us.'

'Uncle stop arguing with that woman, let her leave this compound,' shouted Yvonne who had been listening to the conversation from afar.

'Our mother cannot leave here. This is supposed to be our home as well,' one of the daughters said.

'Shut up, you fool. Who invited you to this case?'

'Me, a fool. Mum, warn her not to insult me because I will give it to her.'

'Jane, keep quiet!' ordered Angel.

'Ok Yvonne, let's leave it at that for now.'

'Before you go Mr Kingsly, I would like to get involved in what is happening. I would like to sit by Mary or at the other side of the corridor. I don't want to sit inside the house like an outsider. Moreover, my family is coming for the burial as well.'

'No problem, we will arrange and see to that.'

The family managed to control the situation till the burial was over. Angel sat in the house and insisted that she must mourn Joe's death according to tradition: she shaved her hair, fasted and cried as much as she could. Her children were with her throughout the one month of mourning and prepared food for her.

The family then arranged a meeting with Angel and her family.

Mary explained that for the past twenty five years she lived with Joe, he had never mentioned that he had children elsewhere. She directed the question to Joe's brother,

'Do you know about this story of your brother having an affair?'

'Excuse me, this is not an affair. To have five children by one man is passed an affair stage. This is a family,' Angel responded.

'No, it is an affair; any union without traditional observance or other necessary services is not recognized in our culture.'

'Don't forget that the blood of Che's family runs in my children's veins. So they belong to this family.'

'Madam Angel, we are not disputing what you are saying, but Joe is no longer here to support you.'

'Yes, but the children have to belong somewhere. They are his children.'

It was then that Peter spoke,

'Madam Angel, we have been trying to make meaning of your presence in our family. You don't seem to understand how difficult it is for us to accept your story though it may be true. We are not saying that you are a liar. But it looks like we have to follow the legal procedure in this case to clear everyone. You need to get your papers and your lawyers and we will settle this in court. Your legal right as the second wife will be established. You have not shown any paper or anything to convince us that these are Joe's children. We are not saying that Joe could not do a thing like this. One can only defend what one knows.'

The meeting ended on that note.

17

Murder Investigation

An investigation of the murder was set by Major Ibrahim. The notion of murder created fear and more confusion among the armed forces as suspicion reigned in the barrack. Nothing of that nature had ever happened before, Major. Ibrahim observed.

Peter asked permission from Major Ibrahim to remove his father's personal documents from the office. It took him a week to go through the files in Joe's office. He worked with Sledge for the first two days. Sledge collected the documents needed for the process of his pension and continued to work on them.

While Sledge concentrated on gathering Joe's documents to start the procedure for his pension, Peter visited the police to continue the murder investigation.

Peter took time to turn every paper in the office. Among other things he discovered, he found two important documents and a thought provoking letter.

In one of the files marked urgent was his father's will which was carefully placed in an envelope in the file. It was dated two days before his untimely death. Peter felt that his dad must have planned to send the document to his lawyer. Peter looked through the points on the will and his attention was caught where it was written:

'My property will be shared among my nine children as follows:

He saw that the names of his children were listed and the amount of money or property allotted to each one stated.

Peter knew that he was not supposed to read the will without the lawyer so he quickly folded the document and planned to send it to the lawyer or rather discuss with him. The claims from Madam Angel began to make sense to him.

'So my father was using his money to bring up another family while neglecting us, his children.'

Anger welled down his throat. He was tempted to drop chasing after murderers, but then remembered his choice not to be influenced by his father's behaviour. He realized that he did not really know his father.

'How could he conceal such a thing from us, more so from his wife whom he loved so much?' Peter wondered. It is true what Shakespeare says … 'One can never detect the mind of men by mere construction of the face,' he sighed and went on to read other documents.

In the same file was the copy of his resignation letter dated two weeks before his death. He also read the letter and there his father said that he had been serving the nation for the past 37 years and his desire was to resign and give an opportunity for the young people. He was aware that the moment was crucial but he had decided to discontinue at that stage.

The third important and controversial letter was among the other papers on his table.

The letter was written by one of his colleagues named Major General Abudullah. The name rang a bell in his head but he was not clear where he had heard that name before. He read the letter.

Mr Joe,

I heard you are resigning too. You have been proving to be clever since I knew you. You want to join the contest group for presidency. Well you know that you are putting your hands into the lion's mouth so be ready to receive the obvious result. You snake.

Signed

Abudullah.

He read the letter again and again trying to make sense out of it. He folded the letter and deposited it inside his inner pocket and continued his packing. He searched for a reply or something that could help him understand whether his father had said anything in connection with politics or the forth coming election, but found none.

He never heard his father discussing politics. Could it be that Major General Abudullah suspected his resignation and the 'obvious result' was death?

His father may not have taken that threat seriously and hence the reason for the letter lying carelessly on his table.

'My father cannot believe that anyone would have killed him though he could be stubborn,' Peter thought.

He tactfully inquired at home about the name without revealing his objective.

'Yes, I have seen him once when I was sacked from my first job in Yaoundé. He is our father's colleague.' Sledge revealed.

'He never got on well with your dad,' their mother added.

Then Peter remembered that it was the man their father described as a 'Social Chameleon.' He nodded and kept quiet. He had to keep his suspicion to himself till he got more proof. He was not sure how to go about it. He planned to contact his father's lawyer about it as well.

Peter duplicated the letter and left a copy in one of the official files in the office, but he retained the original copy.

When he went to the office the next day, he felt that someone had entered the office. He discovered that the file that contained the letter was missing. Other files were scattered on the table. The person must have gone through the files before he saw the one he wanted. He had been taking pictures of how he left the office each day since he started the clean-up. So he took a picture again before he went in search of Major Ibrahim to report his findings.

'Peter is everything ok?' Major asked as soon as he saw him.

'Yeah, it's just that it seemed to me someone entered the office yesterday after I left because one of the files I left on the desk is missing. I left eight files on the table and when I came back they were scattered and one had disappeared.'

'I did not send anybody there. What could have happened? Who is interested in those documents?'

'The missing file contained some of the correspondences between my dad and Major General Abudullah. Who is he?'

'Major General Abudullah is in charge of 120 battalions in Mfoum Division. The police have been working with the investigation to uncover the mystery but their findings are not enough to establish what really happened. I have released the gate men on bail but they are still suspects. I need to clear those files now. How much time do you need to clear your father's personal belongings?'

'I am almost finished. I feel we need to contact the police handling this case to take note of this incident.'

'Yes, you are right; who ever took the file must be connected to the story.'

Peter took the letter to their family lawyer. He saw the letter as a serious threat. They planned to send people to Major General Abudullah since he did not come for the burial to officially tell him about Joe's death. The people must note his reaction and tape whatever he says. Two men were hired and they went to Mfoum and asked to speak with Major General Abudullah. They did not disclose the object of their visit till they arrived at his office.

'What can I do for you?'

Please Sir, we came to tell you that Mr Joe Che passed away a month and some days ago. Searching among his friends, we discovered that you were not there at his burial and we felt obligated to come and officially tell you.'

'No, no , there is no problem. Actually, it is eh Major Ibrahim whom he worked closely with. Normally, since he was not in my jurisdiction, I did not feel obliged to attend his burial. Yeah I heard of it.'

'But Sir, he listed you among his friends.'

'No, there is something wrong then, Joe and I were never that friendly and I do not wish to discuss this matter further.'

'Thank you Sir for giving us audience.'

' Em who sent you?'

'Oh it is the family.'

'Ok, good day.'

The messengers went back to the lawyer and Peter and narrated their observations.

'When we mentioned Joe's name he was taken by surprise. He frowned and pretended to remain calm but one could see that he was struggling not to show his true self. He was not sympathetic at all. In fact, he was nonchalant and less interested about the whole issue. When we hit the nail on the head, he decided to dismiss us.'

'Thank you for your discoveries and observations. I will pin him down on his words and in connection with his letter when the time comes.' The lawyer explained. 'He had confirmed that they were not friends and he was not obliged to come to his burial even though they were colleagues.' Peter was convinced that Abudullah had a hand in his father's death. But he has to find evidence to drag him to court. He was to be monitored.

The police had told Mr Ibrahim not to dispatch the things in Joe's office as they needed more investigation. They questioned Peter about his discoveries and asked for his private letters. Peter gave them the copy of Abudullah's letter. The missing file had not been forgotten. More interrogation from the gate men revealed that the man they saw jump out of the gate was a tall fellow. He had no gun in his hand but as he fell out on the other side of the fence he took to his heels without looking back and boarded a taxi that waited for him. The taxi had a Yaoundé plate number YND 4...

Peter wanted to find out if there was a camera. They remembered the camera and went for it. They wondered why no one had thought of it till then. The camera captured the number plate of the taxi and the half face of the man though it was half hidden with his cap. Peter felt that the face looked familiar but he could not tell where he had seen the face. The driver's face was not clear. So the police started searching for the face and the plate number. That meant searching everywhere in the country. After six months of endless searching, the police were unable to locate either of the two people or the vehicle.

One day Peter went out with his friends for a drink in an off- license bar. He overheard a group of men shouting and arguing loudly. Even though the people he was with were talking as well, he strained his ears and overheard something strange.

'You are a fool to challenge me. I have done things that no police would ever find out because it was directed from the headquarters,' one of the men said.

'You people from Yaoundé, I do not doubt you at all because you people have the lives of others on your palms.'

'Yes we set the pace and others follow. Do not make an attempt to create another party because one by one we shall eliminate them as we did with Mr Che and others.' The man was drunk and continued to wave his hands like one selling his father's land.

Peter recognized the voice and looked hard again. He was sure it was him.

Ngong and his group moved out of the pop arguing loudly and as usual Ngong's voice toppled the rest in his boast. Peter followed him from a distance. Meanwhile he rang the police. The police responded immediately and came. When Ngong and his friends saw the police coming they ran in different directions but Ngong was half drunk and could not run fast like others he was taken by the police. Ngong continued to talk because the drink was in control of him.

'I'm supposed to be dead by now. The foolish man told me to get lost after eliminating that fool. He wants to close up all the evidence but I couldn't do that. I no want die.'

'Who is the man?' asked the police. Two policemen were on his sides now guiding him along.

'The foolish Major General Abudullah.'

'Who did he ask you to do away with?' It was then Ngong looked up. Fear gripped him.

'Who are you? What do you want?'

'It is okay, come with us gently so that we do not hurt you.'

175

'Who are you? Are you sent by Major General Abudullah to end my life?'

'No we will not hurt you; we want to make sure you are not hurt again by him.'

Ngong was interrogated at the police station and he mentioned three high army officers that had used him to assassinate their enemies. Major General Abudullah sent him to kill Mr Joe Che. He was paid much money on the ground so that he would kill himself after he had carried out the job. He could not comprehend how he accepted to do such a nasty job to a man who was his friend's father. His jealousy about what Peter had become was the driving force. He wanted to hurt him but not by killing his father.

The investigation team, together with the lawyer and Peter compiled the evidence. Ngong was life evidence and Major General Abudullah's letter was the second point. They took into cognizance that since it was a murder case, it must be public. People were interested to know how the murder case was discovered. The normal procedure for the accused and the accuser was performed by the police. Peter was the accuser and Major general Abudullah was the accused. His arrest was televised.

As soon as the date of the trial was announced, Peter was optimistic that things would turn out well. Hundreds of journalists from across the country began to visit the barrack and their home to gather information.

18

Court Marshall

The trial took place in Mesong-Mesala high court. The courtroom could not hold more than the key participants: the three Judges, the nine Jurors (four on one side and five on the other side). The family of Major General Abudullah was on one side and Joe's family on the other side. Behind the window was the public prosecutor. Facing the judges and the jury were the lawyers, on the window side and the counsel for the victim, on the other side the counsel for the accused and lastly, the accused himself. More than five hundred army officers came to witness the case. Some people were surprised and were still in doubt that Major General Abudullah who was friendly with everyone could be accused for murdering his colleagues. More than 300 had requested press accreditation, but as there were only fifty places available in the press gallery, it would turn out that those without seats could watch in an adjoining room, where the proceedings were relayed non-stop on video screens. The trial ran from 1st of August until 13th of October, much longer than planned. Three hundred police had been drafted in as security.

Ngong was seated at the other end with his family away from Major General Abudullah's family. He looked over the desk to the opposite side where the lawyers sat. His eyes could not see clearly. He screwed them again. The air in the room was heavy for him. His eyes rested on one of the lawyers at the other end.

'No it is not him, he is outside the country, it could be his brother but then he had no other brother.' Fear held him. 'He will cut his pound of flesh today,' he thought. He was the accused. He did the killing knowing him well. He panicked. A tap at the back reassured him. It was his sister Jessica. He turned to her briefly.

'Can I speak in the vernacular, I am afraid I may not speak correct grammar.'

'No, nobody will hear you, try and speak pidgin.'

'I am scared; I think Peter is there among the lawyers. He will not forgive me. I am doomed.'

'Who is Peter?'

'He is my accuser …'

The magistrate called for order. The case was about to begin.

Mr Abudullah denied writing a threatening letter to Mr Joe. He explained as calmly as he could master the courage.

'Mr Joe and I were never friends. So I could not have thought of writing a letter of that sort to him. I am aware that he did not like the way I was.'

'When you heard about his assassination, how did you take it?'

'It did not mean anything in particular to me because it has nothing to do with me.'

'You did not think that Mr Joe wanted to resign and compete with you in the political context?'

'Well, I am not aware of such things going on. I am not interested in politics.'

'Mr Abudullah, on the 13th of February, exactly five days before the assassination of Mr Joe, you wrote a letter to him and signed it. I have the original copy with me here.'

178

'No, there is something wrong somewhere. You could not have got the original letter because everything was removed before the office was evacuated.'

There was a murmur in the court and the jury called for order.

'Mr Abudullah, tell the court what you know about the missing file that contained the letter.'

'I have no clue of what happened there. I was in Yaoundé.'

'How did you know that the original letter was gone?'

His lawyer interrupted, 'I feel that the question is highly technical for my client. He has said he does not live in Bamenda. I object. 'Objection overruled,' Mr Peter continued.

Mr Abudullah denied any knowledge of writing a letter to my father but he had the knowledge that the original copy was removed. It would be interesting to let the jury and the court know that a week after my father's death I got permission from Major Ibrahim to remove my father's personal documents. My sister, Sledge and I worked in the office for a week and I discovered the letter written to Mr Joe signed by Major General Abudullah. I photocopied it and kept the copy in the file while I retained the original copy. On coming the next day to continue my work the file was mysteriously missing.

'You, son of the bitch, I am not the only Major General Abudullah at the barrack, shouted Mr Abudullah.

In the same file I saw Mr Joe's resignation letter and his will.

'Mr Abudullah, there is a young man sitting directly opposite you, look at him. Do you recognize him?'

'No I have no idea who he is.'

'The young man whose name is Ngong revealed that you sent him to assassinate Mr Joe.'

'The man is mad. Why listen to him? How can you call me murderer?'

'That man has done some work for you in the past.'

'He is confused between jobs.' He faced Ngong, 'you should be dead by now.'

'Mr Abudullah what type of jobs did he perform for you?'

Interruption by his lawyer, 'this is not required in this case.'

'You paid him heavily to assassinate Mr Joe and kill himself after that to destroy the only evidence. You thought he was dead. Now I invite Mr Ngong to tell the court the arrangement between him and Major General Abudullah.' Peter sat down.

It was on the next hearing that Ngong gave a full story of how he met Major General Abudullah and had been working for him for the past six years. He saw how desperate Ngong was looking for a job. He called him and gave him employment under the oath of secrecy: to monitor and sabotage the opposition party and to fetch him any information about their plans and dealings. Then he eliminated those that may be in the plan. Major General Abudullah thought that Mr Joe wanted to retire to join the opposition party and he was seen as a threat.

From the evidence of Major General Abudullah in the court, his responses and reactions revealed more than the eyes could see. He knew about the removal of the file from Joe's office.

Ngong was given 50years imprisonment and Major General Abudullah received life imprisonment.

People who attended the case thought that Peter was clever and tactful in his discoveries. Three weeks later, Peter received invitations to join the bar association. He was registered as a practitioner with a full right to work anywhere in the country.

19

Another Side of the Coin

It was a very rough road. There was no one in view on the doggerel road that created a doleful feeling as Peter wangled his way through the slippery potholes that occupied the road. The potholes were a welcome wage to stop vehicles from slipping down the ditch on both sides of the road. Abandoned cars were a common sight and most of them headed towards the ditch. One wondered how the people from that vehicle came out. Down the road, there were few people struggling with their car trapped in mud. They looked like people who had been buried and brought out from the grave. The road was really a death trap. There were a number of vehicles that had fallen inside the ditch. One could hear the crippling sounds of Curlews on the trees. The bad road and the fear it created forbade one from enjoying the singing of birds. There is often the mingling of good and bad things in life. They are like coins with two sides.

'Is there no better way to go to this village? We may lose our limbs by the time we arrive at the end of this journey,' Sledge inquired.

'That is the only road that leads to the village. I have committed myself to do this. I would have asked the man to come and see me in Nanga- Eboko but I know it would be giving away the secret and he would not come.'

'Who is he and what is the secret?'

'Oh, he is the man who took Angel's first son. When our lad died, the woman could not cope with her children. She sent her son Mark to live with a man who claimed to be her saviour. The man boasted that he had helped many children but actually he used them for trade and barter and treated them worse than slaves. It sounds weird. Angel has struggled to bring her son back but the man blocked any contact with Angel. It is difficult to come here as you can see.'

'How did you know this?'

'Angel has come to my office several times and asked me to help her recover her son, so I decided to help. I do not know the man but I have his picture and her son.'

'This sounds like a risky task to accomplish. And the road is horrible. How did she send a child to this kind of place?'

'Well she has never been there herself. The place is far and the road is a difficult place to travel in this rainy season. It is like the road from Cameroon to Nigeria.'

'I heard that people sleep for weeks on that road pushing and pulling trapped cars especially during the rainy season.'

'It is rainy season now and I am not sure what will happen when we arrive there. We have to take the man by surprise or else he will hide the child. According to Angel, people told her that the man is planning to abduct the boy from the village to where no one knows.'

'Why must you undertake to do this for her? It sounds like a dangerous adventure.'

'Well we can only do what we are able to do. I have the warrant to get the local police if he proves impossible, but I hope it will not get to that.'

Peter danced his way down the road. At the middle of the road, just close to the other vehicle that got stuck, his car could not move. The right front wheel tire went inside the pothole and got stuck. It could not be jerked out. Peter came down, brought out his shovel and repair materials. He went inside the bush, cut branches of trees and laid them down

184

close to the car. He invited the other group to help him pull the car. They came and lifted it up, allowed it to rest on the tree branches. Peter went inside and drove it with force and landed on the opposite direction of the road. He drove it to a temporal safety space. He joined them to push their own car. Their cloths were covered in mud which made them look like people from the grave. Peter brought a small gallon of water from his car and they washed their faces and hands and boarded their vehicles and the wangling journey continued. Just a few kilometres away from there, there was another vehicle in more serious trouble. The left front tires had flown right inside the ditch. Their spare tire was not good enough. They were left with the option to buy and replace the tire. The two vehicles could not help with their spare tires because their tyres would not fit into theirs. The car was higher and of a different mark.

'You have saved the first group but I feel sorry for the second group. They would sleep in this place today.'

'People have been sleeping on this road. It is slippery and difficult to walk upon as well. It is obvious that people who live in these villages are trapped during the rainy season.'

'How do villagers get the food they eat?'

'They are farmers. They have food but it is difficult to transport the food items to town. They are not really bothered by what is happening outside their world. It is a backward area. Education is very poor here. People spend their time only in the farm and drink a lot.'

'I have been hearing about bad roads but I never knew that road could be such a death trap.'

'We were lucky to meet those people; we would have been trapped as well. Two of us could not have pulled out the vehicle.'

'It is true. What will happen if darkness meets us here? I am scared.

'We have no option but to wait for dawn or else we would land in the ditch.'

'The ditch is very deep. One can hardly see the depth of it.'

'No, I will not dare to look. The story was told about a young tourist who fell inside and was never seen again.'

'Oh that is sad really.'

'He was warned not to go near the edge, but no one knew what happened and he was gone.'

They were almost out of the dangerous part of the road. The atmosphere was humid and rain seemed to be eminent. Peter and Sledge were grateful that they were out of the hostile road though their car was covered in mud. One could scarcely recognize the colour of the vehicle, but then they were faced with the mission at hand- how to locate the man and the boy.

They asked a passer-by about the village. There are ten clans that make up the village. The man belonged to the warrior clan. The passer-by did not know the man in question but he directed them to the village. It was dark when they arrived at the clan. They spent the night in the vehicle.

Early in the morning, just before farmers were up to go to the farm, Peter traced the man's compound. It was a thatched house in an isolated area. Few huts built with bamboo woods and plank could be seen in a distance. On the right side of his compound were plantain and banana shrubs. The other side contained all kinds of rubbish beside the local made toilet. It looked neglected. He knocked at the door

'Na who,' the voice came from within.

'Oh na some man wey e want tok for you.'

'You comot from wu sai?'

'I comot from warrior clan. Na my name be Nupe.'

The door opened and a middle aged man came out and closed the door behind him. He was very thin and spent with a large wrinkled face. He was shocked to see the strange faces. Fear settled in his face as he tried to speak correct English.

'Y-es what can I do for you.'

'Please are you Mr Joan.'

'Yes, what do you want and who are you?'

'Peter brought out his warrant of arrest.

'Yes I am from Yaoundé and I have the warrant to arrest you and bring you to Mfoum.'

'Arrest me, for what?'

'When you arrive in Mfoum, you will know.'

'I won't go to Mfoum I have nothing to do there and besides I have no means of going.'

'I came with a car, pointing at the car parked just outside his compound.' Mr Joan looked straight and saw the car. His fear increased. He called,

'Mark, trouble dee for here,' and he continued in the vernacular language that sounded really foreign to Peter and Sledge. They were not sure what he said to Mark.

Mark came out of the house. He was all bones and lanky. He yawned and greeted us. One could see that Mark was malnourished and ill.

As they were looking at Mark and wondering what next to do, the man ran behind the house and jumped his little fence and disappeared from the scene. Peter used the opportunity.

'Mark your mother sent us to come and rescue you. Your mother's name is Angel. I am your half-brother and this is my sister. So come with us quickly and then we will not arrest him again. What we want is your safety. Your mum wants to see you.'

'My mum, she did not come with you?'

'No but she is waiting for you. Come, there is no time to waste as we are not sure what he has gone to do.'

So they moved quickly out of the house taking Mark with them.

Mark was dumfounded, weak and could not say much. They offered him the leftover food to give him little strength and he slept most of the journey.

'How did you get that name Nupe?' asked Sledge

Peter laughed 'no it just occurred to me that he might be suspicious, I quickly thought of that local name. You remember one of those who helped us pull the car on the road was calling one of them Nupe.'

'Yeah it is true, I forgot all about that. You were too fast for Joan.'

'Yes, he had no chance to smuggle Mark away with him. He left him to strangers and ran for his life.'

'He is weird. People like him exploit the ignorance of their victims.'

'Often nemesis catches up with them.'

At this time they arrived at the spot where they met the second group whose tire went off into the ditch. They were still there waiting for a good Samaritan. So the driver joined them to get another tire.

'We have been there for two days and we are not sure how long it will take me to get another vehicle travelling to this direction,' the driver explained.

'So you have to buy food as well when coming back.'

'Food would be the first thing and then the vehicle to bring me back here. You are our saviour so far.'

'Where are you from?'

'I am from the warrior clan. I used to take people to and from the market to sell their produce once a week.'

'So you ply this road every week?'

'Yeah, that is the only road to Town.'

'You must be made of iron.'

'What can we do? He laughed, 'we are used to it.' 'We can go without food for days before we arrive at the village.'

'That sounds hard.'

'Well since the government neglected us, we do not see ourselves as part of Cameroon. We hardly get signals to listen to radio or watch television.'

'So there is still a place like this in our country,' Sledge was surprised.

'We are in-between two valleys, it is difficult to get the waves but people are happy and peaceful and law abiding. You can leave you door wide open and no one will get in or steal. Villagers are friendly with one another. We tolerate one another, joke and laugh together. We take life really simple. Very few people own cars or what you will call decent houses, but people are generally happy with their life's situations.'

'You must be proud of it after all.'

'Oh I love it here. It is only the road that disturbs people, though ironically many people would not want the road to be repaired or tarred.'

'Why not?'

'The nurse fears that foreigners might come in to trade here and change the simplicity and peace of the village. There is no development without crime.'

'Well, you are right, but development expands your horizon and brings something new. 'Some people may find it difficult to change from their way of life to another, but I am sure some people would like a change.'

'We all like a change but we do not like the negative aspect of the change.'

'You need education for your children.'

'Yes we do, it will take time for education to come here. Our leaders are tactful in allowing organizations in, but the Christian societies seem to be making a move on that line.'

The driver alighted in Bafoussam while they continued to Furawa.

When they arrived back at home, Angel thought it was a dream. She wept at the sight of her son. She blamed herself for sending him away and said that she would never send him to live with anyone again. Peter felt sorry for the young man and felt a responsibility to take care of Angel's children.

'Peter be cautious. You have your life to live. Yvonne warned.'

'Well, you are right. I'll do what I can. Angel and her children need help though. I cannot fold my hands and look on. Dad is gone.' What is life other than what you are able to do? It is my choice to give help where I can. Peter changed the discussion.

'What is the situation between you and Ben?'

'Well, Ben made several efforts to connect again after his aborted visit with his parents but nothing happened. Right now I have moved on with another man.'

'What of your son.'

'What about him.'

Will he follow you to your new found love?'

'I have not thought about it. Mum feels that he can stay with her and attend school. I know that Ben is interested in him. I am not sure what will happen. I'll wait to see.'

'Sledge got engaged with a guy at the social insurance.'

'I like the guy. He is cool and funny. He made mum laugh the day he visited.'

'I am glad for my sister. I am planning to visit Kelly in Nigeria. She is in her third year.'

'Wait till her graduation, then I can come with you.'

'I will go again when graduation comes. I like to visit Nigeria.'

'It is one of my dreams.'

'Angel is in the house. She came to talk with Mum.'

'She looks worried,' Peter observed.

20

The Beginning of the End

Angel came to see Mary. She looked devastated like an abandoned old vehicle.

'I came to plead for clemency in the way I jumped into your family. Now I realize that you and your children are very understanding, accepting and objective.'

'You came to plead for mercy. How did you get to know Joe?'

'I broke up with my boyfriend. It was a very painful experience and I swore that I would never live with any man. But then I wanted to have children. I love children. Joe picked me up on the road one day. He was interested and he asked about my life. We began from there really. He told me he was married but that was not considered at the time as I was attracted by his kind gesture. I began to accompany him on his long trips. I became pregnant because I wanted to have a child by him. He really cared for me and the child. Then it happened again and again till I had five children. I wanted to come in then as his second wife but he would not allow that. He loved you and he respected you. I did not know you but I was jealous of the position and space you occupied in his life. I routed the idea of remaining in the background but, that was the only option he gave me if he would continue to take care of the children and me. Joe brought meaning back to my life. When he died I thought it wise to take the opportunity to establish myself in his home.'

'I suppose we all need love and a sense of belonging. He lived a lie to me. It would have been better for me to know where his money went. Here we are.'

'I know, I lived a lie with him and that is why I feel you deserve to know the truth no matter how late it is. I look at your lovely home and intelligent children you have and I feel ashamed of my behaviour. I wish I had met you before he died. I do not know what would have happened but I know I treated you badly.'

'We are on our own now facing the reality of our lives.'

'I wish I could turn the clock back, she cried.'

'Life experiences are the best teacher and our choices are our personal couch.'

'I have no family. My parents are dead and the two brothers of mine have continued their life regardless of what happens to me.'

'So what do you want from me.'

'I am pleading that my children and I should be taken as your own. I cannot contribute much but I have realized that I need you and your children in my life. Peter underwent a very rigorous journey and rescued my son. No one could have done that for me without requesting for a pound of flesh. Sledge was very open and honest in the court and granted my children their rights. What else do I need other than to ask to be given a place in your heart despite my cunning way of entering it?'

'I suppose Joe had played his part and gone. I will speak with my children and come back to you.'

'Thank you.'

Mary called her children and tabled before them Angel's request.

'On what ground does she want to belong to us? queried Yvonne

194

They reflected and Sledge spoke next

'I feel that we need to be open about this. What do we lose if we take her in? I mean we are all grownups and will soon leave home. Mum will need a companion when we have all gone. I see it as providential that she lives with her and accompany her in her aging stage. We take care of her and her children as much as we can. They are our half- brother and sisters now. Circumstances have increased our family and we cannot do anything now.'

'I think I buy Sledge's idea. Let us show people that the world is a playground which people abandon when tired. It is likened to the saying from the Book, *Power of Now* by Eckhart Tolle. It says:

'The world is like children playing by the ocean who build sand-towers with constancy and then destroy them with laughter. But while you build your sand-towers the ocean brings more sand to the shore, and when you destroy them the ocean laughs with you. He ended by saying that the ocean laughs always with the innocent. Dad is gone and we are innocent of his secret life. Nature has a way of mending what is destroyed by human frailty.

'I feel that we will lose nothing really now, so let us welcome them,' expressed Kelly.

'My children, you are a blessing to me. I am of the same opinion as you. Yes, I need companion and friends to love. Two wrongs cannot make right but one right has the power to repay more than two wrongs. Having said this, I forgive your father and welcome Angel and her children as part of our family.'

So the old life ends where the beginning of a new one starts.

Mary recalled the old poem she had learnt as a young girl. It was written by Minnie Louise Haskins and titled 'God Knows.' it reads:

'And I said to the man who stood at the gate of the year;

'Give me a light that I may tread safely into the unknown.'

And he replied:

'Go out into the darkness and put your hand into the hand of God that shall be to you better than light and safer than a known way.'

So I went forth, and finding the hand of God, trod gladly into the night. And He led me towards the hills and the breaking of day in the lone East.'

'Mum you never recounted this poem before,' Sledge pointed out.

'Yes, this poem was written in 1908. It is very old, but the idea of trust in God remains powerful. I feel it is my trust and my faith that carries me all through my life. We need to regain our spirituality.'

'You are right Mum,' Peter came in. One of my surprises when I was in United Kingdom was that many people have turned away from their faith. They brought the notion of God to us and then many of them turned away.'

'Faith and belief are evolving. Time will come when they will turn round again.'

'Do you think so?'

'Yes I do.'

Angel and her children came and lived with Mary and her children. She became a wonderful companion to Mary when her children got married and began their new homes. Peter eventually got married to Irene and they settled in Nanga Eboko.

Questions

Chapter One

1)   The family of Joe is in confusion; discuss this in relation with the exchange between Mary and Joe in chapter 1.

2)   Describe the characters of Peter and his friend Ngong.

3)   Examine the political situation as observed by the students in this chapter

Chapter Two

1)   How did Mary try to protect her family problems from outsiders?

2)   Describe Peter's disappointment with his father.

3)   What are the practical steps Peter takes to continue his aspiration?

4)   Why was peter sent behind the bars and how did the story end?

Chapter Three

1)   Describe Joe's Character and his attitude towards his family.

2)   Why did Mary's father take Mary home from the Hospital?

3)   Give an account of how Joe was pardoned by Mary's father.

4) Why did Peter want to challenge his father?

Chapter Four

1. Describe Yvonne's understanding about friendship.
2. Give an account of Yvonne's relationship with Ben.
3. Was Yvonne abandoning her home to live with Ben justified? Discuss this in relation to her father's rejection of Ben.
4. How would you describe Peter's intervention in rescuing his sister, Yvonne?
5. Why did Mary decide to take care of her grandson?

Chapter Five

1) Describe Sledge's experiences with Mr Tom.
2) Compare and contrast Sledge's and Joy's character.
3) How would you describe Mr Tom's character?
4) What lesson do you learn from the story of the Wolf and the house dog?

Chapter Six

1) Describe the problems Peter encountered in his effort to enter the University.
2) Give an account of the encounter between Ngong and Peter.
3) Examine the students' unrest as it concerns the medical department at the University of Buea.
4) Examine the part Peter played in the riot.

5) Describe the character of Miss Ode and how Peter handled the issue between them.

Chapter Seven

1) Describe the situation at the social insurance according to Sledge.
2) How did Sledge try to help some people at the social insurance?
3) Why was Sledge transferred to Yaoundé?
4) Describe the situation she found at the pension department.
5) Why was Sledge sacked from the social insurance?
6) Describe the character of the Managers.
7) Festus is a fickle minded person, do you agree?

Chapter Eight

1) Describe Ben's approach to Yvonne
2) Why did Yvonne react negatively when she saw Ben?
3) Describe the character of Cecilia.
4) Analyse how Yvonne's family received Ben's request.

Chapter Nine

1) Describe Ben's family.
2) Why did Ben decide to involve his parents in his issue with Yvonne
3) Give an account of Ben's second visit to Yvonne.

Chapter Ten

1) Examine Peter's journey from Buea to Bamenda.
2) Describe the political situation in Cameroon drawing points from Ngong's political party.
3) Why did Ngong dislike Peter?
4) What suggestions did Peter give Yvonne concerning the letter from Ben?

Chapter Eleven

1) Discuss the meeting of Ben and Yvonne in this chapter.

Chapter Twelve

1) What are the key points discussed by Peter, Kelly and Sledge in Yaoundé?

Chapter Thirteen

1) Describe the meeting of the families of Frank and Joe.

2) Examine the characters of both families?
3) How would you rate Joe's treatment of Yvonne in this chapter?
4) Was Joe's refusal to Frank's request justified? Discuss

Chapter Fourteen

1) Sledge stands as an ideal Manager, discuss.

Chapter Fifteen

1) Describe Peter's experiences in London?

2) What are the qualities of conduct which Peter admired and why?

3) Analyse the telephone conversation Peter had with his friend, Gerald.

Chapter Sixteen

1) Describe the disaster that struck Joe's family.

2) Analyse the appearance of Angel into the family of Joe.

3) How did the family handle Angel's case before and after the burial?

Chapter Seventeen

1) How was the murder case uncovered?

2) The way you make your bed, so you lie on it. How true is this statement in regard to Ngong?

Chapter Eighteen

1) Narrate the issues raised at the court.

2) How would you describe Mr Abudullah's character?
3) The power to make a choice is within. Discuss this statement in connection with Ngong, Abudullah and Peter.

Chapter Nineteen

1) Describe the journey to the village.
2) How did Peter and Sledge rescue Mark from Mr Joan?
3) Describe the reconciliation between Angel and Mary's family.
4) Life is full of surprises, discuss.